"There was nothing I could do. All I did was defend myself."

Q: "All right, Ms. Lehane, calm down. We get the picture. Let's just go over it one more time. Now you say that . . ." the detective began.

A: "I'm tired. We've gone over this and over this. I want to go home. You said I could go after I answered a few questions. That was hours ago."

Q: "A man's dead, Ms. Lehane. He died in your apartment. We're just trying to get to the bottom of what happened."

A: "You know what happened, you just don't believe me. I don't think I should answer any more questions."

Q: "You agreed to be questioned by the police, Ms. Lehane. You waived the right to counsel."

A: "I've changed my mind."

Dear Reader,

When two people fall in love, the world is suddenly new and exciting, and it's that same excitement we bring to you in Silhouette Intimate Moments. These are stories with scope and grandeur. The characters lead lives we all dream of, and everything they do reflects the wonder of being in love.

Longer and more sensuous than most romances, Silhouette Intimate Moments novels take you away from everyday life and let you share the magic of love. Adventure, glamour, drama, even suspense— these are the passwords that let you into a world where love has a power beyond the ordinary, where the best authors in the field today create stories of love and commitment that will stay with you always.

In coming months, look for novels by your favorite authors: Kathleen Eagle, Marilyn Pappano, Emilie Richards, Heather Graham Pozzessere and Kathleen Korbel, to name only a few. And whenever—and wherever—you buy books, look for all the Silhouette Intimate Moments, love stories with that extra something, books written especially for you by today's top authors.

Leslie J. Wainger
Senior Editor and Editorial Coordinator

MAURA SEGER

Sir Flynn and Lady Constance

SILHOUETTE·INTIMATE·MOMENTS®

Published by Silhouette Books New York

America's Publisher of Contemporary Romance

SILHOUETTE BOOKS
300 East 42nd St., New York, N.Y. 10017

SIR FLYNN AND LADY CONSTANCE

ISBN: 0-373-07404-2

First Silhouette Books printing October 1991

All the characters in this book have no existence
outside the imagination of the author and have
no relation whatsoever to anyone bearing the same
name or names. They are not even distantly
inspired by any individual known or unknown
to the author, and all incidents are pure invention.

Books by Maura Seger

Silhouette Intimate Moments

Silver Zephyr #61
Golden Chimera #96
Comes a Stranger #108
Shadows of the Heart #137
Quest of the Eagle #149
Dark of the Moon #162
Happily Ever After #176
Legacy #194
Sea Gate #209
Day and Night #224
Conflict of Interest #236
Unforgettable #253
Change of Plans #280
Painted Lady #342
Caught in the Act #389
Sir Flynn and Lady Constance #404

Silhouette Desire

Cajun Summer #282
Treasure Hunt #295

Silhouette Special Edition

A Gift Beyond Price #135

Silhouette Books

Silhouette Christmas Stories 1986
"Starbright"

MAURA SEGER

and her husband, Michael, met while they were both working for the same company. They have been married for seven years after a whirlwind courtship that might have been taken directly from a romance novel, and Maura credits her husband's patient support and good humor for helping her fulfill the lifelong dream of being a writer.

Currently writing contemporaries for Silhouette Books and historicals for Harlequin Books and mainstream, she finds that writing each book is an adventure filled with fascinating people who never fail to surprise her.

Prologue

Police Headquarters
85th Precinct
New York City

Transcript of Interrogation
Subject: Lehane, Constance
Time: 4:30 a.m.
Case: #475890-B, Sheffield, Lewis, deceased

Question: "What time did you return to your apartment, Miss Lehane?"

Answer: "Shortly before 10:00 p.m."

Q. "You invited Mr. Sheffield in?"

A. "Yes, I already told you, we'd had a pleasant time at dinner. I asked him in for a drink."

Q. "You'd never been out with him before?"

A. "No, this was our first date."

Q. "So you asked him in. What happened then?"

A. "We talked for a while. He indicated that he wanted to... sleep with me. I was surprised."

Q. "Why?"

A. "This was a first date. We hardly knew each other."

Q. "Come on, Miss Lehane. You're a very attractive woman, and you did ask him in. Didn't you expect him to express at least some interest in being intimate with you?"

A. "He didn't 'express some interest.' He went a whole lot further than that. Over dinner, he was very easygoing, very pleasant. Once we were in the apartment that changed. He became much more aggressive."

Q. "How so?"

A. "He started trying to touch me and began speaking very graphically about us... being together. I tried to let him down lightly, make a joke out of it, but that didn't work. When I told him to leave, he refused. We struggled."

Q. "You did nothing to lead him on?"

A. "No, absolutely not! All I did was go out to dinner with the man. That's hardly an invitation to rape, is it?"

Q. "You did more than just go out to dinner. You invited him into your apartment. He didn't force his way in there, did he?"

A. "No, but I told you, he changed. He became very violent. I was terrified. He was much stronger than I am."

Q. "Yet he's dead, and you're alive."

A. "He slipped on the rug! He hit his head on the corner of the marble coffee table. There was nothing I could do. All I did was defend myself!"

Q. "All right, calm down. We get the picture. Let's just go over it one more time. Now, you say that..."

A. "I'm tired. We've gone over and over this. I want to go home."

Q. "Sure, as soon as we get this done. You say..."

A. "You said I could go after I answered a few questions. That was hours ago."

Q. "A man's dead, Miss Lehane. We're just trying to get to the bottom of what happened."

A. "You know what happened, you just don't believe it. I don't think I should be doing this anymore."

Q. "You agreed to be questioned, Miss Lehane. You waived the right to counsel."

A. "I've changed my mind. I want to go."

End of transcript

Chapter 1

Rain again. Dank, soggy, under-the-collar rain that perfectly suited Flynn Corbett's mood. He stepped out of the chauffeured limousine that had brought him to work, avoided the oil-slicked stream rushing past the curb and headed into the Park Avenue building that housed his offices. In the elevator he shook the water from his thick black hair, and wondered about the odds of getting away for a few days in the sun. His caseload was a little lighter than usual; he just might be able to manage it. The thought cheered him up slightly.

The elevator stopped on the thirty-seventh floor. He got out directly into the reception area of the law firm of Dickinson, Rosenbaum, Corbett and D'Angelo. The walls were adorned with original art, the carpet was thick enough to drown in and the furnishings had cost more than anybody cared to admit. All to drive home to prospective clients a single, unassailable fact—breathing the rarified air of New York's most successful private law firm could get very expensive very fast.

"Good morning, sir," the receptionist said. She was tall, blond and polished from the top of her stylishly coiffed head to the bottom of her calfskin-clad feet. Her features and figure were perfect. Before going to work for the firm, she'd been employed by a top-flight plastic surgeon who had thrown in free work as part of her compensation. Every time Flynn looked at her, he was reminded of a trip he'd made to Disney World with his niece and nephew. The twins had had a hard time telling the robots from the people. Sometimes Flynn did, too.

"Morning," he said, and strode on, passing the picture of Dickinson—the firm's founder—who, although long dead, was still glowering. On the other side of a heavy oak door was the inner sanctum, home to the partners and their various clerks and secretaries. Flynn's office was at the far end, on a corner that commanded a view north along Park Avenue and East and continued across the river into the borough of Queens.

There were two other such offices on the same floor. One for Bob Rosenbaum, who handled strictly corporate work, and the other for Chuck D'Angelo, who did divorces and real estate. Which left the good stuff for Corbett himself, at least that was how he saw it. There were others who would have disagreed. Some attorneys thought criminal law beneath them, usually because they found it scary and far too stressful. Flynn loved it. He reveled in the primal fight of guilt versus innocence. It had taken him to the top of his profession and made him the envy of his colleagues, had paid for a life-style that had been beyond even his wildest dreams while growing up in Hoboken on the other side of the river and the universe.

That was the good part. The bad part was that sometimes—like now—it stank. He'd lost a big case the previous week, and the defeat still rankled. An appeal was planned, and he was convinced his client would be exonerated eventually, but that wasn't the point. The point was that he hated to lose. Hated it with the same passion that he loved the law and justice. There were no halfway measures with him. One of these days he'd learn to relax, take things easier, chill out, et cetera. And one of these days he'd be dead. As far as he was concerned, they were both the same.

"Good morning, Mr. Corbett." Helen McWhirter rose from behind her desk, notebook in hand and a no-nonsense look in her eyes. She was fifty-five and plump, with steel-gray hair she never bothered to dye and a face that could only be called plain. She'd been married thirty-two years to a man who adored her, had five children anyone would have a right to be proud of and was looking forward to the arrival of her first grandchild later in the year. She took no guff from anyone, least of all Flynn Corbett. If he had any secrets she didn't know about, they didn't count for much.

"There's a lady waiting to see you," she said, stressing the word 'lady,' which was one she didn't use all that often.

Flynn frowned. "I thought my first appointment wasn't until ten." He'd been looking forward to having the time until then to wade through the pile of paperwork on his desk.

"She said it was extremely urgent. I thought you wouldn't mind." As she spoke, Helen—or "the McWhirlizer," as she was known by the lesser lights around the office—glanced pointedly at the newspaper on her desk. It was the day's *New York Times,* the only paper Helen read. Flynn, by contrast, wallowed in all the tabloids, the *Wall Street Journal* and anything else he could get his hands on. He was one of those people who got the deep twitchies if he didn't have a constant, steady supply of reading material. Content didn't necessarily matter just as long as he had *something*.

Even the staid *Times* had its moments. A headline in black, heavy type ran across several columns at the top of the front page:

Lewis Sheffield Found Dead

Scion of Influential Family Killed in Quarrel

Flynn had read the details over breakfast. Or rather, he'd read three versions of them—the *Times*'s and the more flamboyant versions presented in the city's two tabloid newspapers. Personally he thought the tabloids had the edge on this one. At least they made it sound a whole lot more interesting than the *Times* did.

"When did Miss Lehane get here?" he asked.

"About an hour ago," Helen replied, ignoring his attempt to preempt her. "I gather she hasn't slept. I gave her some coffee and put her in your office to wait."

"Very considerate of you," Flynn said dryly. It wasn't like Helen to fuss over the clients, but every once in a while she'd take one under her wing. Her instincts were good; she'd never yet gone to bat for a guilty party. They'd have to see if the averages held.

"Okay," Flynn said, "hold all my calls."

Helen nodded. She allowed herself a satisfied smile before sitting down again behind her desk.

The tabloids had described Constance Lehane as being "in her late twenties, tall, redheaded." The more enterprising of the bunch had even managed to secure a photo of her taken at a recent business event. In the picture she looked cool and confident.

Seated in the visitor's chair across from Flynn's desk, she looked anything but.

"Miss Lehane," he said as he walked toward her. She jerked nervously and stood up, smoothing her hands on the gray skirt she wore. Her eyes were blue with dark circles under them. The hair the reporters had described as red was actually closer to auburn and looked mussed. Her lips were pale and her skin cold, but her handshake was still firm.

"Mr. Corbett?"

"That's me. I understand you wanted to talk." He gestured for her to sit down again and took his own place behind the wide chestnut desk. All the while he continued to look at her assessingly. Worn-out as she was, and scared to boot, she was still a remarkably beautiful woman. She had that extravagant perfection of feature and form nature sometimes bestows for no apparent reason except that it wants to. But more than that, there seemed to be an actual person looking out from behind the large, wide-spaced eyes. He caught a gleam of intelligence and vulnerability that made as much of an impact on him as her more obvious attributes did.

"I appreciate your seeing me without an appointment," Constance said softly. Despite the coffee, her mouth was dry. She looked at the man opposite her and felt a shiver of apprehension. He wasn't what she'd expected. Given his reputation, she'd presumed that he'd be attractive in the smooth, impervious way of successful men. She hadn't counted on the aura of rugged masculinity he exuded, the hawklike features, the linebacker's body and especially the amber eyes that seemed to see straight through her. No wonder Flynn Corbett was such a potent presence in the courtroom. He had her wowed and he'd barely said a word yet.

He stared across the desk at her and said matter-of-factly, "You've had a tough night."

"And a worse morning. Have you seen the papers?"

"Sure have. The *Times* played it pretty straight, but the rest had a field day. The Sheffields are a powerful family in this town. They've got a lot of money and influence."

Constance nodded, relieved that she didn't have to spell everything out for him. "I guess I should have thought of that right away. But I was so frightened I just didn't know what to do."

Flynn leaned back in the big desk chair. He folded his hands together and stretched out his long legs in the attitude of one prepared to listen. "Suppose you tell me what happened."

"If you've read the papers, you already know most of the details. Lewis Sheffield and I met in the course of business. He runs—he ran—a private movie production company and was looking for someone to promote his films. He hired my company and they assigned me to the account. We saw each other professionally off and on for about a month. When he asked me out to dinner, I didn't have any reason to refuse. He seemed . . . very pleasant.''

Flynn resisted the impulse to note that Sheffield was also very rich and very unmarried. In short, up for grabs. He'd let her tell it her way.

''We had a nice evening,'' Constance went on. ''At least, I thought we did. Lewis was very cordial, easy to talk with, that sort of thing. When he took me back to my apartment, it seemed only natural to invite him in for a few minutes.'' Her voice rose slightly, becoming firmer. ''I asked him in for a drink, that's all. Nobody sleeps with someone on the first date anymore. Aside from the moral issues, nobody would be crazy enough. I had no reason to think he'd expect that.''

''He'd given you no indication of what he was thinking?''

''No, none at all. He seemed like the perfect gentleman.'' She tried to laugh, but the sound came out more like a sob. ''That's such a cliché but it's true. I was totally unprepared when he insisted we sleep together. And when he grabbed me, all I could think of was that this can't be happening. Not to me, not in my own apartment with somebody I know. It was all so crazy.''

''What happened then?'' Flynn asked.

''We struggled. He was very strong, more than you'd think just by looking at him. I've never been so frightened.'' Her eyes darkened as she relived the memory. ''I really thought I wasn't going to be able to stop him. He let go of me for a second and raised his arm as though he was going to hit me. He took a step forward and suddenly he slipped. When we'd started struggling, the drinks were knocked over onto the rug. It was wet and when he stepped on it, his feet must have gone right out from under him. Anyway, he fell and hit his head on a corner of the marble coffee table. For a moment I just stood there. I didn't know what to do and I was so afraid he'd get up again. But then when he didn't, I bent over him. He looked unconscious, only when I tried to find a pulse, I couldn't. There was very little blood, but he was dead all the same."

"What did you do when you realized that?"

"I called nine-one-one and told the operator who answered what had happened. She took my name and address and told me to hold on. The paramedics and the police arrived within just a few minutes."

"Did the police question you immediately?"

Constance nodded. "A little, but then they asked me to come back to the precinct house. I wanted so badly to get out of the apartment, away from where it had happened, that I agreed. They had me wait for a while and then they started asking more questions."

Flynn straightened up in the chair. "Did they tell you that you had the right to have an attorney present?"

Constance nodded. "I didn't think I needed one."

"Why not?"

"Because I hadn't done anything wrong! All I did was defend myself, and besides, it was an accident. In hindsight, I realize I should have insisted on a lawyer anyway. They just kept asking me the same questions over and over until finally I told them I wouldn't answer any more.''

"How long did this go on?"

"I'm not sure exactly," Constance said. "It was after midnight when we started, and I stopped it around four-thirty."

"You talked to the police for four hours without a lawyer being present?" Flynn demanded incredulously.

"I told you, I didn't do anything wrong. Besides, I was brought up to respect the police. I didn't think I had anything to fear from them."

"That's not the point. In this town you don't sneeze without a lawyer being present. To be blunt, Miss Lehane, you come across as being very naive."

"Maybe so," Constance said stiffly, "but the last time I checked that wasn't a crime."

"It ought to be," Flynn muttered. "All right, what's done is done. Can you remember what you told them?"

Constance looked puzzled. "Of course I can. I told them the truth."

"I mean the details, where you went to dinner, what you ate, what he said, what you said, whether he was drunk, whether you were—"

"I wasn't and neither was he. We shared a bottle of wine over dinner but we didn't finish it."

"What about at your place? You said there were drinks."

"One drink each and they were barely touched. Nobody was drunk."

"What about drugs? Any chance he was on something?"

Constance shook her head. "No, he seemed perfectly fine."

"Until you got back to the apartment and he went through this big, dramatic change."

She stared at him, her eyes wide and luminous against her ashen face. "Yes," she said brokenly, "until then."

Flynn sighed. He was getting a bad feeling about this. The Sheffields had a lot of friends in places that counted, and Constance Lehane's story was just begging to be picked apart. No wonder the cops had kept her so long.

He stood up abruptly and strode over to the windows. Thirty-seven stories below, the life of Manhattan went on. Cars crept along, people scurried around them, horns blared, sirens wailed. Constance Lehane lived in New York. If the papers were to be believed, she had a fairly high-level position with a major advertising agency. Yet she'd acted like some Iowa farmer's daughter on her first trip to the big city.

Or so she said.

"I charge four hundred and fifty dollars an hour," he said. "If you're indicted and we go to court, I require a retainer of twenty thousand dollars."

She gasped. When he turned around, the color was back in her face, with a vengeance. She stood up a little shakily. "I'm sorry," she said. "Obviously I've been wasting your time."

"Sit down," Flynn said.

"You don't understand me. I'm not pleading poverty. I've got a good job and I've saved some money. But I can't possibly afford you."

He walked around to the other side of the desk, closer to her. "Sometimes," he said, "I make exceptions. We'll talk money later. First I'm going to make a few inquiries on your behalf. While I do that, I suggest you lie low. The media will be watching your apartment by now, so pick out a nice, unobtrusive hotel somewhere and check yourself in for a few days. When you're settled, let Helen know where we can reach you."

He picked up one of the files on his desk and opened it. "That's all."

When she was gone, he reached for the phone and depressed the intercom button. Helen picked up immediately. "Get me Morgenstern," he said.

He ignored Helen's cluck of approval and looked again at the file. It failed to hold his attention, but then he hadn't really expected it to. Constance Lehane had made sure of that.

Chapter 2

Outside on the street in front of the building, Constance paused to get her bearings. It was still raining hard. People streamed past, huddled under their umbrellas. Traffic crawled along bumper-to-bumper. Technically it was spring, but winter was lingering. A sharp wind came off the river, blowing straight at her.

She shivered and pulled her raincoat more closely around her. Her own office was five blocks to the north. She could be there in minutes. But then what? Could she face the barrage of questions and worse yet, the looks that would undoubtedly be waiting? Exhausted as she was, the mere thought was daunting. There was a pay phone on the corner. She dodged through the crowds to reach it and shut the door quickly. Her hand shook as she punched in the number. Phil Stevens answered on the third ring.

"Yeah?" For Phil, that was being cordial. He wasn't a man to waste words. Fifty years old and a former Marine, he had taken a small, nondescript advertising agency and turned it into one of the country's top hot shops for hard-hitting campaigns. Along the way he'd assembled a formidable talent roster whose members boasted they'd go the last mile for him. Phil drove his people hard, but when the crunch came he was always there for them. Constance was counting on that now.

"Phil, it's Constance. I need to talk with you—"

"Where are you?" he interrupted.

"At a pay phone a few blocks from the office. I don't know if you know—"

"You bet I do. The phone's been ringing off the hook. Every media type in New York is trying to find out about you. What the hell happened?"

Briefly she told him. When she was done, his response was short and to the point. "What do you need?"

Constance closed her eyes, fighting the wave of relief. She couldn't afford it yet. "Thanks, Phil," she said quietly.

"For what?"

"Believing me."

He was silent for a moment before he said, "I do, kid, but I know you. A lot of people don't. Some of them are going to see this differently."

"I know." She took a deep breath. "I think I'd better not come in for a while. I've seen a lawyer who's advised me to lay low."

"Better listen to him. Who is he, by the way?"

"Flynn Corbett."

Phil grunted. "Good choice. I met him once at some political thing. He doesn't pull any punches."

"I'll say," Constance murmured a little ruefully. She still felt bruised by the encounter. Better not to dwell on it. "There's a lot of work on my desk: the Broadside video, the Chemise ads, that perfume concept you wanted and some other stuff. I'll arrange to have everything messengered to me and stay in touch so the schedules aren't affected."

"I don't expect you to keep working at your usual clip while this is going on," Phil said. "Fact is, it probably wouldn't be a good idea to try. You want to do one or two things, that's fine, but some of your work is going to have to be reassigned."

"I fought hard for all those accounts, Phil—you know that. I don't like losing them even temporarily."

"Those are the breaks, kid. The accounts are yours and they stay that way, but somebody else is going to have to pinch-hit for a while. That's no reflection on you, it's just the facts."

"All right," she said reluctantly. His decision didn't surprise her. Realistically she couldn't expect to produce the caliber of work that she would under normal circumstances. And he had assured her that it would only be temporary. With some people, she would have doubted that, but not with Phil. He kept his word come hell or high water.

Still, she hung up with the lingering thought that this was only the beginning. Flynn Corbett had called her naive. Maybe there had been some truth to that, but she was wising up fast. Lewis Sheffield might be dead, but the effects of what he had done were still very much alive.

For a moment she was tempted to throw caution to the wind and go back to her apartment. It was the closest thing she had to a home, after all, and she deeply resented being hounded from it. But realistically the last thing she needed was a confrontation with the media. Her best bet was to stay out of sight and hope they lost interest fast.

A bus pulled up at a stop near the phone booth. Constance ran for it through the rain, jumping on just as the doors were about to close. She dropped her fare in the collection box and found a seat toward the back. A young, nicely dressed man across the aisle smiled at her.

Her stomach lurched. For a moment she seemed to see Lewis Sheffield again. She turned away quickly and stared out the window.

The bus plowed north in fits and starts. She got off at Seventy-ninth Street. There, facing the avenue, was a small hotel little known to the general public but favored by those who appreciated comfort and discretion. Constance walked into a lobby furnished with eighteenth-century antiques and made her way to the small reception desk.

"May I speak with Mrs. Fairley?" she asked.

The young woman behind the desk hesitated. "Are you a guest?"

Constance shook her head. "I'm a friend of hers." Gently, knowing how Dominique's employees tended to protect her, she added, "I think she'll see me. My name is Lehane."

Fortunately the young woman did not appear to have read the morning papers. At least, she gave no sign of recognizing Constance. She disappeared into the back office and returned almost immediately, looking relieved.

"Mrs. Fairley says you're to go right in."

Constance thanked her and went around the reception desk to the door behind it. It opened onto what was really a spacious office but looked more like a drawing room in an English country house. Dominique Fairley was sitting on the chintz-covered couch. She was a tiny woman with blue-black hair, coffee-hued skin and bright, vivacious eyes that belied her sixty-five years.

Born into desperate poverty in the rural South, she had triumphed over seemingly insurmountable obstacles to become one of the world's great prima ballerinas. After almost two decades on the stage, she had made a brilliant marriage to a British diplomat and returned with him to England. Upon his death, she had remained in England for a while before deciding that New York was where she belonged. Lacking any immediate family, she had poured her considerable talents into the hotel, making it a centerpiece of elegance and grace.

Two years before, she had gone out to visit a nearby tailor who was fitting a dress for her. On the way back she suffered a shortness of breath and collapsed on the street. The young woman who rushed to her aid, got her to the hospital and stayed with her until the danger was past was Constance Lehane. They had been friends ever since.

"I'm so glad you're here," Dominique said as she held out her hand. "I've tried to reach you, but there's been no answer at your apartment."

"I was only there for a few hours this morning and I left again very early."

The older woman nodded. "Sit down, dear. I'll ring for tea and something a bit more substantial. You'll be staying, of course?"

Constance hesitated. Now that she was here with Dominique she felt reluctant to involve her friend in her troubles. There were other hotels, after all. The problem was how to identify herself. She would have to use her real name, if only because most decent hotels required a credit card even from those who said they intended to pay with cash. Which meant that, sooner or later, she'd be recognized. And she dreaded what that would mean.

"If it won't cause any problems," she said finally. "I don't think it will be for very long. This ought to be straightened out in a few days."

Dominique did not reply directly. She merely nodded and said, "I'll have a room prepared immediately. You'll need some things, too. One of the staff will pick them up for you. In the meantime you're going to have a cup of tea, a nice long soak and a good sleep. Everything will look brighter once you've done that."

Constance managed a smile. "It sounds as though you speak from experience."

"Absolutely. There is nothing tea, bubble bath and sleep can't cure. My late husband always said that."

"Francis took bubble baths?" Constance asked. She'd only seen him in photographs, but she had a hard time imagining the tall, wiry Englishman with the pencil-thin mustache stretched out in a sea of froth.

"He was devoted to them," Dominique replied. "He said whatever had been good enough for Churchill was good enough for him, and I can't say he was wrong." She paused for a moment, picked up the phone and spoke briefly into it. When she was done, she said, "Now, tell me what you've done so far about this dreadful situation."

"I went to see Flynn Corbett this morning."

Dominique's eyes widened. She might be in what she referred to as the golden sunset of her life and still in love with her deceased husband, but she wasn't above noticing another man if he particularly merited the attention. She folded her small hands in her lap, settled herself more comfortably against the cushions and smiled. "Tell me all about him."

"I'm not sure where to begin. He's very... tough."

Dominique nodded. "Oh, yes, he is that. Also brilliant, dynamic, sexy, sought after and, so they say, invulnerable, at least to the blandishments of beautiful women."

"Since the last thing I'm interested in doing is blandishing anything at him, that suits me fine."

"Hmm. You do know Cissy Blanchard was absolutely desperate to marry him?"

Constance's eyebrows shot up. The older woman knew everyone and everything in New York's highest social circles. She was a repository for rumor, innuendo, gossip, slander and, ultimately, truth. Perhaps one percent of what she knew she shared. The rest remained firmly locked away where it belonged.

"Cissy Blanchard, really? I thought she was involved with—" She named a well-known real estate developer who specialized in littering New York with yet more gargantuan monoliths that it didn't need.

Dominique nodded. "She is now, but that only happened after she finally realized Corbett was having none of what she was offering. Not that he's a saint, mind you. There have been a number of relationships, rather few actually considering the man himself, but apparently he's *very* selective. Also very busy. They say he eats, breathes and lives law."

"If that's true, he has some funny ideas about it. He told me I was crazy to speak with the police on my own."

Dominique's eyes darkened. "Oh, dear, is that what you did?"

"I still don't see why it was so wrong," Constance said defensively. "I have nothing to hide."

"Of course you don't. But that isn't the point, is it? The police are supposed to doubt everyone. That's how they get to the bottom of things." She patted Constance's hand reassuringly. "Oh, well, what's done is done. The important thing is that you not let this get to you too much. You'll have a nice rest here while Flynn sorts it all out."

Constance resisted mentioning that she hadn't yet figured out how she was going to afford Flynn. The moment she did so, Dominique would insist on paying, and she absolutely wasn't having that. They chatted awhile longer about nothing of any particular consequence. Dominique had a great gift for putting people at ease, even under the most difficult of circumstances. By the time a young man stuck his head in to say that Constance's room was ready, Constance was feeling far more relaxed than she had when she arrived.

She thanked Dominique, received a quick hug in return and followed the young man upstairs. Her room was on the third floor in the back, overlooking a small private garden. The windows were thickly plated to mute the usual city noises. Dominique's English country taste was again in evidence in the big four-poster bed, the flowered carpet and the white lace curtains at the windows. A pottery vase held an unpretentious bouquet of daffodils.

The overall effect was one of space, light and peace. A small refrigerator discretely tucked away in a corner held fruit juice, sodas, wine, beer and snacks. In the adjacent bathroom a thick terry-cloth robe hung on the back of the door. A painted basket contained everything from a toothbrush to bath salts and shampoo.

Constance paused only long enough to put in a quick call to Helen McWhirter, telling her where she could be reached, before deciding that what was good enough for Churchill—and Francis Fairley—ought to be good enough for her. She filled the tub with steaming water, added the bath salts provided and stripped off her clothes. Sinking into the silken water, she almost groaned with relief. She laid her head back against the padded rim and let her eyes close.

Flynn Corbett's mood hadn't been all that rosy right from the moment he rolled out of bed into the soggy day, and it was deteriorating rapidly. More than an hour after asking Helen to get him Ben Morgenstern,

Manhattan's district attorney, on the phone, he was still waiting. At first, Ben "hadn't come in yet," then he "was meeting with associates," then "on another call." Finally Flynn took matters into his own hands. He got on the phone himself with the D.A.'s hapless secretary and spoke to the point.

"Tell your boss to stop dodging me, or the next time I get him on the handball court he'll come away missing a piece of his anatomy he *probably* still has some use for. Got that?"

She got it. So did Ben Morgenstern, who found the idea amusing.

"You and what army, Flynn?" he asked, chuckling, once he got on the phone. "Last time we played, you were huffing and puffing like an old man."

"In your dreams," Flynn replied. "You spend too much time on the hustings. All that chicken and peas makes you fat and lazy."

"You wish. So how you been, buddy?"

"Not too bad. Yourself?"

"Top-notch. Cecilia sends her regards."

Cecilia was Ben's wife, and a good candidate for the world's most patient woman. She had seen her brilliant, ambitious husband through law school and the early days in New York politics, all the way to the office of district attorney, a place where even those who resented him admitted he belonged.

Ben was tough and smart; he had to be to carry the burden of administering justice in one of the highest crime areas in the country. Among his many abilities was a talent for playing the media like a virtuoso violinist. He gave them just enough to keep them purring but never so much that they could predict what he'd do next.

Flynn—who had known him for years and played killer handball with him regularly—liked to think that he could, but there were times when he wasn't sure. Like now.

"I had a visitor this morning," Flynn said. "Constance Lehane. It seems she had kind of a rough time with your boys last night."

The casualness went out of Ben's voice. On a thread of steel he said, "I'm familiar with what you're referring to. In fact, I got a report on it this morning, but she waived her right to counsel. That's right there on the tape and in the transcript. The minute she changed her mind, the interrogation was stopped. She's got nothing to complain about."

"Maybe not technically, but they could have gone a little easier. She'd just been through a terrible experience."

Ben was silent for a moment before he suddenly laughed. "Come on, Flynn, what is this? You're not some tyro legal aid attorney fresh out of law school. You know how we do things. She agreed to go to the precinct, she agreed to be questioned. She was in no physical distress, she hadn't actually been harmed, after all. So there was no reason *not* to take her statement. Everything was completely aboveboard."

"She got the impression your guys didn't believe her."

"Should they?"

"It was an attempted rape, she defended herself and the guy got killed in the process. You won't see too many this cut-and-dried."

"You say so, but I'm not so sure."

Flynn's hand tightened on the phone. They were getting very close to what he wanted to know. "Why not?"

Ben hesitated. Finally he asked, "Are you formally representing her?"

"You bet."

"Then you have the right to review the transcript of the interrogation and any other evidence that may exist *if* a decision is made to proceed. Until then, I suggest you back off."

"I'm not too good at that, Ben. I want to know why you're pussyfooting around on a clear-cut case of self-defense. What's the problem?"

"The problem is that you're pushing too hard. I haven't even had a chance to review the results of the autopsy that was done on Sheffield last night. I want to do that and I want to think things over. Then I'll let you know."

Flynn considered that briefly. Without expression he said, "The Sheffields have a lot of clout in this town."

Ben's voice hardened even further. "I don't like what you're suggesting."

"Neither do I. I'd hate to see you make a major-league mistake."

"I'll worry about that. You worry about your client. Maybe she's on the level and maybe she's not. Until that gets settled, make sure that she keeps herself available."

"I'll give her the message," Flynn said coldly. "Make sure you get mine. Lewis Sheffield tried to rape a woman last night. I have no problem with the fact

that he's lying cold on a slab in the morgue because of
it. Go head-to-head with me on this one and you'll
regret it, Ben.''

"Yeah, well, we'll see. Could be she's pure as the
driven snow. But you know what snow looks like in
this town, Flynn. It's got all sorts of muck mixed up
in it. I suggest you watch what you step in.''

On that note he hung up. Flynn did the same. He sat
at his desk, staring sightlessly out the window while his
mind turned over the conversation. Ben had received
a report on the interrogation as soon as he got to the
office. An autopsy had been performed the previous
night even though the morgue would ordinarily have
been closed at that hour. Like it or not, and despite all
protestations to the contrary, Sheffield's death was not
being handled routinely.

His face grim, he reached for the phone.

Chapter 3

The ringing phone jarred Constance awake. She lifted her head and looked around disjointedly. For a moment she had no idea where she was. Slowly the room came back into focus. Dominique, the hotel, the bath once-steaming now uncomfortably cool. She had fallen asleep in the tub.

Grasping the sides, she pulled herself out and fumbled for the robe on the back of the door. With it on, she got to the phone just as Flynn was about to hang up.

"Where were you?" he demanded without preamble.

"In the tub. I fell asleep."

"Dumb. You could've drowned."

"I know that. It won't happen again. What do you want?"

"To give you a message," he said. "Don't leave town."

"W-who...?"

"Morgenstern, the D.A. I just talked to him." He sighed. "Ordinarily he's a pretty straight guy, but it seems you're an exception to the rule. I'm getting some bad vibes on this."

Constance's shoulders slumped. She sat down on the edge of the bed, gripping the phone. "What do you mean?"

He told her, succinctly and to the point. When he was done, she said, "I don't understand. Why don't they believe me?"

"Right now, I've got no idea. I need to see the transcript, but until there's a clear indication that they're going to the grand jury for a possible indictment, they can stall me on that. Same with the autopsy results." He paused for a moment. "If there's anything you haven't told me, now's the time to do it."

"There isn't," Constance said firmly. "I've told you the whole truth."

"Then there shouldn't be any problem."

"You don't sound so sure."

"I'm not. I'd feel better if we had something more on our side right now. Evidence, for instance. You said that you and Sheffield struggled. Have you got any bruises?"

"No," Constance said quietly. She still ached, but that was as much from tension and tiredness as anything else. "The struggle was brief. He didn't have time to do any real damage." Not the physical kind, anyway.

"That's too bad," Flynn said, half to himself.

"I'm *so* sorry. If I'd realized where all this would lead, I'd have encouraged him to slap me around a little."

He made an impatient sound. "One thing you've got to realize, if this does go any further, is that it's going to be unpleasant. Lots of people will be saying things you won't like."

"I've figured that out already."

"Good for you. Go get some rest. I'll pick you up around 7:00 p.m."

"What do you mean, you'll pick me up?"

"We're going to have dinner together." He had decided so on the spur of the moment, provoked by the weary courage in her voice and the memory of how she had looked sitting in his office. The decision surprised him. Generally he made it a point to steer clear of his clients every way except professionally. He had to if he was going to keep the emotional distance he needed to do his job.

Nothing had happened to change that, except that he suddenly wanted to see Constance Lehane again and do it somewhere away from the formality of his office where she was likely to be most on her guard. Life had taught him not to ignore his instincts. He wasn't about to start now.

Before she could protest, he said, "I need to get to know you better if I'm going to do a decent job defending you. Besides, I don't want you sitting around your hotel room brooding. You'll only get more upset, and then if the D.A. does want to question you, you'll be at a disadvantage."

"I'm not exactly up for a night on the town," Constance said.

"I'm not suggesting one. You're staying at Dominique Fairley's, right? We'll eat there."

"All right." She was still reluctant, but Flynn wasn't alone in his desire to get better acquainted. If she was going to trust this man in what might turn out to be the biggest decision of her life, she wanted to be sure she was right to do so.

"Seven p.m.," she agreed. "Maybe you'll have better news by then."

"Maybe," Flynn said. He didn't add that he doubted it.

Constance slept until late afternoon. She woke when the desk called to ask if it would be all right to bring up a package. A pot of coffee came along with it. She sipped the rich brew in between shaking her head at what Dominique considered necessary for a comfortable stay. In addition to a full makeup kit and hair-styling equipment, the package included a negligee, slippers, lingerie and a classic "little black dress" that all but shrieked Bergdorf's, the very chic, very expensive department store on Fifth Avenue Dominique patronized. Nurturing suspicions that the older woman already knew all about her dinner with Flynn, Constance made a mental note to reimburse her in full.

With plenty of time yet to dress, she stretched out again on the bed and clicked on the television. The early edition of the evening news was just starting. Lewis Sheffield was the top story.

"Police remain unwilling to release much information about the sudden death of multimillionaire Lewis Sheffield," the blow-dried anchor was saying. "The discovery of his body late last night in the apartment of girlfriend, Constance Lehane—''

Cut to a visual of the outside of her building.

''—has left many questions unanswered. Sheffield was an independent movie producer respected by his colleagues, who today expressed their shock at his unexpected demise.''

Cut to a portly man in white turtleneck and bronze gel. ''Lewis was a brilliant innovator, a real film genius. It's impossible to understate the contribution he would have made to the industry had he been permitted to live.''

''Overstate, you turkey,'' Constance muttered. ''If you're going to brown nose, at least do it right.''

''District Attorney Benjamin Morgenstern,'' the anchor went on, ''declined comment when asked if grand jury action was being considered.''

Cut to the broad marble steps in front of the Manhattan District Court Building. The D.A. was of medium height and trimly fit, with thick dark hair and eyes even Constance had to admit were compelling. He nodded cordially to the reporter attempting to question him.

''This office has no statement at this time. The investigation is continuing.''

Back to the anchor in the studio.

''A spokesman for the Sheffield family, which has been active in political and charitable affairs for several decades, said tonight that the family has full confidence in the ability of the district attorney to see to it that justice is done. Efforts to reach Miss Lehane have failed.''

Constance clicked off the TV. She stared at the blank screen. Disbelief filled her. She had the sense of having been wrenched out of her life and made witness to events far removed from herself.

The anchor had called her Sheffield's girlfriend. It sounded so tawdry, and was wrong besides. They'd only had one date, but more than that, the word cast her in a light that could only be damaging. Worse yet was the way Lewis himself was being portrayed—respected by his colleagues, member of an important family, even "a genius." There was no denying that the man's films had been provocative in a hard-edged, demanding sort of way. With hindsight, Constance realized that she should have paid more attention to them.

She got up slowly and went into the bathroom. The mirror above the sink showed a woman whose pale face was dominated by fathomless blue eyes. Despite the rest she'd had, she looked tired and flat-out scared. A terrible sense of her own isolation and vulnerability threatened to close in on her. It might have succeeded if she hadn't determinedly focused her thoughts on Flynn. She didn't have time to wallow in her own misfortunes. She had to get ready for dinner with him.

Doing her hair and makeup, she deliberately avoided looking into her own eyes. The fear would still be there; she knew that. She just refused to acknowledge it. Zipped into the little black dress, she slid her feet into the black pumps she'd worn earlier and surveyed the results. Her hair was shoulder length and naturally wavy. The auburn highlights gleamed softly. The dress was high necked with long sleeves and a fitted waist. It fell to midcalf and should have been as demure as all get-out. Somehow it wasn't.

At 7:00 p.m. on the dot the desk rang to say Flynn was waiting for her downstairs. She took the elevator to the lobby. He was prowling around near the newsstand, tall and lean in an impeccably tailored business suit. As she walked toward him, she couldn't help noticing the number of people, mostly women, who glanced his way.

Flynn, on the other hand, looked only at her. The amber eyes under thick black brows missed nothing. She straightened her shoulders and dug up a smile out of the strategic reserve.

"Hi," she said.

"You're on time, good. Let's go." Without further ado he took her elbow and steered her toward the small restaurant tucked away to one side of the lobby. The restaurant—called La Sylphide in honor of the title role that had made Dominique famous—was in the French style, with impressionistic murals of scenes from the ballet, discreetly separated tables and seating banquettes. The maître d' greeted them with precisely the degree of warmth that acknowledged they were friends of the owner. They were shepherded to a table in a corner half-concealed by a lattice screen. By New York standards the table was the equivalent of a private island.

"Nice," Flynn murmured as he lowered himself into the chair opposite Constance.

"Have you been here before?" she asked.

"A few times. It's a good place to talk. The food's not bad, either."

Since the kitchen regularly drew five stars in every restaurant guide of any note, that seemed a modest enough assessment. Clearly Flynn wasn't the type to indulge in a lot of hype. Either that or he was just real tough to impress. And if Dominique was to be believed—and she always was—Cissy Blanchard and a few others like her had learned that the hard way.

"What's so funny?" Flynn asked. He had caught the small smile flitting across her features, a real one this time, and was curious as to its cause.

"Nothing," Constance said hastily.

"No, come on, tell me."

She sighed and reminded herself to be more careful in the future. "I was just thinking that it really is an ill wind that blows no good."

He sat back in the chair and looked at her. "What made you think that?"

Lamely she said, "Just that it's nice to be here, that's all." Quickly, lest he think she meant with him, she added, "I really like this place and I've hardly ever gotten here for dinner, that's all."

"Okay. Now, what were you *really* thinking?"

"For heaven's sake, don't you believe anything anyone says?"

"I do when they're telling the truth. Your eyes slipped out of focus slightly. It's the first time I've seen that happen. I want to believe that's because it's the first time you've told me something that wasn't true."

He had her. If she continued to deny that she'd been less than straightforward, he'd have grounds for doubting everything she'd told him. Damn the man! He was getting harder and harder to take.

"All right," she said flatly, "I was really thinking that you have a reputation for being very hard to impress and that I am therefore glad I am here with you in a purely professional capacity, that I am not interested in you as a man. Satisfied?"

Flynn looked down at the table for a moment. When he glanced up again, he was grinning. "That's pretty good. You make your point and skewer my ego at the same time. If you're always that blunt, we'll get along fine."

He handed her a menu almost as though it were a reward and picked up his own, becoming instantly immersed in it. Constance was left staring at the gilded pages and wondering if the point she'd just won was her first or her last. She suspected the latter and supposed she should be grateful for it. The tougher Flynn Corbett turned out to be, the better the job he'd do representing her.

"By the way," she said, "have you heard anything more from Morgenstern?"

"Not so far. I'll check in with him tomorrow."

Constance hesitated before she asked, "Is it possible he'll decide by then to just let this drop?"

"Sure, anything's possible. However, if you're asking if that's what I think will happen, the answer's no."

"Why not?"

"Because whatever he thinks about the merits of the case, if he even thinks there is a case, Ben Morgenstern is too smart not to let this play out a while. The law is supposed to move 'with due process.' That's an important concept, the idea that nothing gets done hastily or impulsively."

"Not even when it's clearly right?"

"Few things are ever that clear. Look, why don't we talk about something else for a while?"

"Like what?"

"You, for instance. I meant what I said about wanting to get to know you better. Suppose you tell me about yourself." He looked at her guilelessly, no mean trick for a man who probably had more guile in his little finger than most people had in their whole bodies. "Since this is all purely professional, pretend it's a job interview. Best foot forward and all that."

"Mary Poppins," Constance said automatically. "That's what she always said. Best foot forward, spit spot." Great, her mind was starting to wander. Flynn would decide she was a flake and decline to represent her. How to explain to him—or herself—that he had that effect on her?

"That's a great movie," he replied. "My niece and nephew have the tape. We watch it all the time."

Constance's mouth dropped open. She couldn't help it, though heaven knew she tried. "You watch *Mary Poppins?*"

He nodded. "Actually I think the books are better. There's a bunch of them, you know. Most people think there was only the one, but in fact it was a whole series. I gave them to Tim and Tina last Christmas."

"Tim and Tina are your niece and nephew?"

"That's right. Tim and Tina, the twins. Isn't that cute?" He grimaced. "My brother and sister-in-law are great people, but they have their weak points like everybody else."

He had a family, one that he apparently cared a great deal about. The tough, compelling man she'd met that morning was showing unexpected depths.

"You like children," she said. It wasn't a question. He'd already made that clear.

Flynn nodded unabashedly. "Kids are the best. A lot of work, of course, but still the best."

"So how come you aren't married?"

Oh, boy, she'd done it now. Talk about going out on a limb with a saw in your hand. Just when she'd been absolutely determined not to let anything personal intrude into their relationship, marriage and kids—otherwise known as the Whole Shebang—reared its head.

Flynn looked taken aback for a moment but he rallied quickly. "Never met the right woman, I guess."

"I know what you mean, you can't be too careful, especially these days. Besides, marriage and all that is overrated."

"Your eyes are out of focus again."

"Excuse me while I put on my sunglasses."

"If you do that, you won't be able to see in here. Let's at least order first."

When the waiter had come and gone, Flynn sat back and looked at her. "How old are you?"

"Twenty-eight."

"How long have you lived in the city?"

"Seven years, since I got out of college."

"Did you always work in advertising?"

She nodded. "I started as a junior copywriter and worked my way up."

"Times have been tough in advertising lately. How come you survived when a lot of other people didn't?"

"I'm not sure exactly, but maybe it has something to do with the fact that I work very hard and never cut corners."

"Ever?"

She shook her head and wondered where all this was leading. A moment later she knew.

"Is that why you were out socially with Lewis Sheffield? Just part of doing the job?"

Constance's hands twisted the napkin in her lap. "If you're suggesting," she said grimly, "that I was trying to use him as a way of furthering my career, you couldn't be further off base. I would never do anything that stupid. Nothing's more guaranteed to get a woman the worst possible reputation in business."

"People will still wonder. In a situation like this, you have to be conscious of public opinion."

Constance thought back to the news broadcast she had seen. "You're right," she said softly. "I've already had a dose of that."

"How so?"

"I caught the early edition of the news. They led with the story." Her mouth tightened. "They called me his girlfriend and basically made him out to be a saint."

"What station was it?"

When she told him, he sighed. "You know the Sheffields are the majority stockholders there?"

Her eyes widened. "I had no idea of that."

"I did a quick check before I left the office this evening. They're heavily invested in a couple of dozen television stations nationwide. They also hold a substantial interest in—" He named the parent company of a major national newsmagazine. "They were major contributors to the mayor's campaign, also to most of the city council, all the congressmen and both of this state's senators. The governor is a personal friend of Lewis Sheffield's brother, who, incidentally, may be our biggest problem. It's a toss-up whether that honor will go to him or his mother. You can bet they're going to be tied in a dead heat.''

"I think I should tell you," Constance said, "that when I get really nervous I tend to eat. At the rate this conversation is going, this could turn out to be a very expensive dinner."

"That's okay, just save room for dessert. They do a great mocha mousse. So you came to New York straight out of college and went into advertising. Before that, where did you live?"

Constance sighed. At the rate he was firing out questions, it might not matter how hungry she was. She'd be lucky if she got a chance to eat any dinner at all.

"Ohio," she said. "I grew up in a little town called Marietta on the Ohio River near West Virginia."

"There's a good college there."

"That's right, but I still wanted to get away, so I went to William and Mary, then New York and you know the rest."

"Not exactly but it can wait. Let's stick with Marietta for a while. Are your parents still alive?"

Constance nodded. "Dad runs a Mazda dealership, Mom does a lot of volunteer work."

"Brothers or sisters?"

"One of each. Jim works for a software company in Seattle. Marjorie lives across the river in Parkersburg with her husband and two kids."

"What have you told them so far?"

She hesitated. Looking down at her plate, she said, "Nothing."

Flynn twirled a fork between his blunt fingers. Light gleamed off the sharp silver tines. "Why not?"

"It doesn't seem right to worry them. They were never too happy about my living in New York in the first place. This will just seem to confirm all their worst fears." When he didn't comment, she added, "Besides, there's no point. They won't understand what happened and they certainly won't be able to do anything to help."

"Okay."

"They're wonderful people, really. This is all just a little beyond them."

"If you say so."

"You think I should tell them."

"I think they're going to find out anyway, and it would be better if it came from you."

Constance sighed. He was right, of course; she just hated admitting it. Part of her was still hoping the whole horrible mess would blow over. He was telling her it wouldn't. "I'll see," she said.

He took a sip from his water glass. Through the etched crystal his hand looked large and tanned. He didn't seem like a man who spent most of his time at a desk. Energy fairly flowed from him.

"So you went to William and Mary," he said, "and then you came here. Do you like New York?"

This was safer ground, less personal somehow. She gave the standard answer. "It's kind of a love/hate thing, you know?"

He laughed. "Yeah, I know. Ever think about leaving?"

"Only every other day. Every other minute since this happened."

"Postpone it until we get straight with Morgenstern. In the meantime, do you have any close friends here?"

"There's Dominique..."

"I mean somebody closer to your own age. Somebody in a better position to really understand what you're feeling and help support you through it."

Constance thought for a moment about the people she knew. They were mostly business colleagues. Like a lot of New Yorkers, her life revolved around her work. It didn't leave much time for anything else.

"I used to," she said softly. "Her name is Deborah Shaw. We were classmates all through college and we landed jobs in New York at the same time. But she got married six months ago and her husband's company transferred him to England. Anyway," she added quickly, "I wouldn't be very comfortable crying on somebody's shoulder."

Flynn's reply was noncommittal. It left her with the feeling that he thought before this was all over she'd be doing exactly that. Her resolve stiffened. She was determined to prove him wrong. The best way to do it was to turn the tables.

"How about a little equal time here?" she asked. "I'd like to know more about Flynn Corbett. What makes you such a hotshot trial lawyer, for instance?"

He grinned. "Is that what I'm supposed to be?"

She nodded. "The terror of the courtrooms. Prosecutors tremble at the mere sight of you. You're the avenging angel of the innocent, the man judges respect and juries adore. That's pretty impressive stuff.''

"It's bull. I'm good at my job for the same reason you're good at yours. I work hard and I don't cut corners.''

"You're being too modest," Constance said. "It doesn't suit you. In fact, you could hurt yourself that way.''

His teeth flashed whitely as he laughed loud enough to make people at several tables turn their heads to look. Unabashed, Flynn said, "Okay, you got me. When I was a kid, the one thing I wanted to be was a gunslinger. Other kids would be playing Superman, Davy Crockett, stuff like that. Not me. I was always the guy in black getting off the train in some dusty western town.''

"Is that where you come from, out West?" She could see him in some wide-open stretch under endless sky, someplace big enough for the man and the spirit he contained.

"Sort of. I was born and raised across the river in Hoboken.''

Hoboken? It was a pleasant enough little town with its share of nice folks whose only misfortune was living in the overwhelming shadow of New York. If she'd ever thought of them at all, she presumed that people who came from places like that had to grow up with tremendous inferiority complexes. How could they not when all they had to do was glance up to see how small they were?

Not Flynn, however. Whatever else he'd brought out of Hoboken, it wasn't a sense of his own relative diminuitiveness. There was something else, though, a hard-edged conviction that power and pomp didn't count for all that much. He spent his life defending individuals against the government, about the most powerful and sometimes the most pompous entity in existence. Some of his clients were pretty powerful themselves and paid extravagantly for his services. But others weren't.

"You must be offered more cases than you could possibly handle," she said. "How do you decide which ones you'll take?"

"Instinct. I have to believe, at the very least, that there is reasonable doubt of the charges being brought against the person being true."

"You don't have to believe he or she is innocent?"

Flynn shook his head. "That's a common misconception about criminal lawyers. It's not our job to determine guilt or innocence, but by the same token, I won't take on someone I flat-out believe did whatever they're being accused of. They're entitled to representation for sure, but it doesn't have to be by me."

"That's reassuring to hear," Constance said softly.

He shrugged, diminishing the significance. "You haven't been charged with anything."

"Not yet."

"No," he agreed, looking at her over the rim of his glass, "not yet."

They sat in silence for several moments before the waiter intruded with their orders. He hovered over them solicitously before being convinced that they had everything they wanted. Whatever had caused the bleak looks on both their faces was apparently not his to either regret or remedy.

When he was gone again, Constance picked up her fork and knife resolutely. The food looked marvelous, and she absolutely wasn't going to let it go to waste. Besides, she'd meant what she said to Flynn—when she got nervous she got hungry. At the moment she was ravenous.

"I'm on temporary leave from my job," she said, "so I won't have much of anything to do until this gets settled. I hate being at loose ends. If I'm going to need a defense, and it looks as though I will, to at least some extent, I'd like to help build it. Suppose you tell me how I can help?"

Flynn hesitated briefly. There were clients who were better off involved with building their own cases and there were those who weren't. Constance was smart, self-disciplined and gutsy. He judged she'd do all right.

He glanced down at the fillet of beef on his plate and decided it wouldn't do any harm to let it cool a little. "Okay," he said, "here's what I want you to do...."

Chapter 4

Constance came down the steps of the New York City Public Library at Forty-second Street and Fifth Avenue. The day was brilliantly clear, and there was an added bounce in people's walks. A soft breeze blew south from Central Park, redolent of fertile earth and budding things. Spring had arrived, tardily, but welcome all the same.

She blinked in the sunlight, trying to clear her head. She'd been in the library since it had opened more than six hours before. Her neck ached and her eyes burned, but she was pleased with the results she'd gotten. She hoped Flynn would be, too.

With an hour to spare before their appointment, she walked the distance to his office. By the time she arrived, her head had cleared and she felt better than she had in several days. Helen smiled when she saw her.

"You're looking much improved, Miss Lehane. Got a good night's rest, I hope?"

Constance nodded and hoped she wasn't blushing. She had slept unexpectedly well after her dinner with Flynn, but once or twice she'd half awakened from dreams she knew involved him.

Helen shepherded her into Flynn's office with a motherly air and suggested a nice cup of coffee. Constance declined with thanks. Flynn wasn't there yet; he was on his way back from court, Helen explained.

Constance barely had a few minutes to get her bearings before the office door flew open and he strode in.

Sternly she told herself not to be an idiot. The man positively could not smell of the untrampled wilderness, of pine forest and pristine lakes, when he had just come from lower Manhattan. Her imagination was running away with her. Yet understanding that didn't change anything. She was suddenly, vividly conscious of him as a man. And more, she was conscious of desire, something she had frankly not thought to feel so soon after Sheffield's attack. The realization stunned her.

"Hi," he said as he shoved his briefcase under his desk. He was wearing another of the dark, well-tailored business suits he seemed to favor. When he took off his jacket, she caught a glimpse of plain old buttons on the shirt cuffs, no fancy links. His tie was also plain and clipless. He loosened it, sat back in his chair and regarded her steadily.

"So how are you doing?"

She swallowed hastily and fought to repress the thoughts trembling through her mind.

"Fine, thanks, yourself?"

"Peachy."

He didn't elaborate, and she didn't ask him to. Instead, she said, "I've got a lot of information on Sheffield. Want to hear it?"

He nodded. "Shoot."

Constance looked down at the notes she'd been reviewing while she waited for him. Her forehead wrinkled slightly as she struggled to decipher her own handwriting. She'd been excited to find so much material so quickly, and her hasty jottings reflected that.

"Sheffield was born in April, 1957," she began, "in Greenwich, Connecticut. He attended various private schools there until he was fourteen, at which point he went to the Hawkins School, also in Connecticut. He left the following year and returned to Greenwich proper, where he attended the public high school. From there he went on to Yale, but again he didn't stay very long. He ended up at New York University, from which he eventually graduated. Sheffield belonged to various professional and social organizations, basically the kind of thing you'd expect of someone from his background. Over the years his name has been linked with half a dozen women in the society pages, but more recently he seems to have been involved with a girl named Delia Russell. She was a debutante two years ago, so she's very young. Her family is old-line, involved in banking and oil. There seems to have been some expectation that she and Sheffield would marry."

"I take it you didn't know anything about her?" Flynn asked. His eyes were narrowed. He was trying hard to take in everything she was telling him, which wasn't easy considering that all he could think about was how great she looked. What was that word—luminous? Yeah, luminous.

Constance shook her head. "No, I didn't. He never mentioned her or anyone else."

"The Hawkins School is one of the top prep schools in the country," Flynn said, dragging his attention back where it belonged. "I wonder why he couldn't hack it there or at Yale?"

"Maybe it just wasn't what he wanted. It looks as though his family may have been trying to program him to suit their own expectations. He could simply have rebelled."

"He could have," Flynn agreed, "or it could have been something else. Is that it?"

"Just about. He founded Stellar Productions three years ago and made three films, which received generally good reviews but not much in the way of distribution. He seems to have been financing the venture out of his own pocket."

"He could afford it. The Sheffields are one of those families who got over here before most anybody else and wasted no time grabbing whatever they could. They've done a damn good job of holding on to it, too."

"So I gather," Constance said. "It's impossible to determine the full extent of their holdings, but they're a whole lot wealthier than I thought. For people with that much money, they live quietly. Most of their efforts seem to be devoted to charity."

"Their *public* efforts," Flynn corrected. "They're very active politically, but it's mostly behind the scenes. The Sheffields belong to the school that says if ordinary folks ever find out how really great it is to have that much money, they'll try to take some of it for themselves. So it's smarter to keep a low profile and make it look like they're giving it all away. In fact, they're wealthier now than they've ever been. Charles Sheffield, Lewis's older brother, is a lawyer. He manages the family fortune, and he is one sharp operator."

"You mentioned that," Constance said. "You also said something about his mother?"

"Elizabeth Burlington Sheffield. She comes from an old Southern family with a respected name and not much else. Ever since her husband died twenty years ago, she's run the show. Charles is tough, but he takes his orders from her."

"Where did all that leave Lewis?" Constance wondered.

"That's what we're going to find out. You've made a good start, but we've got to go a lot further. By the time we're done, I want to know him almost as well as I know myself. Most important, I want to know if what happened in your apartment really did represent a sudden change in the pattern of his behavior."

"I told you, he seemed completely different when we were in the restaurant."

"That's not what I mean. Anybody can come across as a nice guy for a few hours, long enough to catch a woman off her guard. But his family's going to claim that he was strictly Mr. Straight Arrow. They're going to say it was impossible for him to do what you say he did. We have to be prepared to deal with that."

"How?" Constance asked softly.

"With facts," Flynn replied. "There are two ways this can go—either he suddenly acted out of character or he didn't. If he did, there has to be an explanation for why, some kind of change in his life that caused him to behave in a way he would normally have never even considered."

"What could do that? As I said, I didn't have any sense that he was on drugs or anything like that. That kind of thing is pretty hard to hide."

"Usually it is, but there are people who manage it. Besides, there are subtler causes for sudden changes in personality. A few months ago I was asked to represent a man accused of an unprovoked attack on a co-worker. There wasn't much doubt the guy had actually done it, but his wife claimed he couldn't have. She said he was absolutely nonviolent, as decent as the day is long and so on. Plenty of people were willing to testify that she was telling the truth—we had character witnesses up the kazoo. But there were also a dozen witnesses to the actual attack who were ready to swear he *had* done it. It was my job to reconcile the apparent contradiction."

"How?" Constance asked softly. The look on his face—thoughtful, determined, patient—gave her a new understanding into how he worked. He wasn't a man for the quick fix but would pursue a problem doggedly until he had it solved. He was tough in his judgments but also tolerant and giving. No wonder she felt safer with him than she had in a very long time. And no wonder that scared the living daylights out of her. She wasn't prepared for those feelings just now. Not so soon after Sheffield. Not at this point in her life. It wasn't in the cards, on the schedule, whatever. Or was it?

"It turned out," Flynn went on, oblivious to her thoughts, "that six weeks before the attack the defendant had been in a car accident. His head went smack into the steering wheel, and he ended up with a bad bruise on his forehead, but otherwise he looked okay. Only he wasn't. The neurologist I hired found out there was damage to the frontal lobe, the part of the brain right behind the forehead that seems to have a lot of control over personality."

He summed up succinctly. "My client got the treatment he needed, the judge got the facts and the end result was not guilty by reason of diminished capacity. Now I'm not saying there was necessarily anything similar in Sheffield's case, but if he suddenly changed his behavior, there had to be a reason."

"If," Constance repeated. "You also suggested it might not have been a change."

Flynn nodded. "He was thirty-four years old. If he had the capacity in him to commit an act of violence, the odds are long that he didn't keep it pent up inside all that time. He would have done something else before now."

"There's never been a hint of anything like that about him. His movies were violent, sure, but no one ever suggested he was capable of violence personally."

"Which brings us back to the very wealthy and powerful family."

Constance's eyes widened. "A cover-up? You're suggesting that what happened to me happened to other women in the past and the family hushed it up?"

"I'm suggesting a possibility," Flynn said, "nothing more. We've got to look at all the angles." Quietly he added, "And we've got to do it fast."

Constance's stomach tightened. "Why?"

"I ran into Morgenstern this afternoon at the courthouse. What he had to say isn't good. Apparently he feels the autopsy report is inconclusive."

"It can't be," Constance protested. "What happened was so—" she broke off, searching for the right word "—so clear, so obvious. He fell and hit his head once—how could the autopsy miss that?"

"It didn't. The medical examiner agrees that Sheffield died from a single blow to the head. The problem is how the blow occurred. The M.E. says the nature of the wound, the angle and so on, simply isn't conclusive enough to determine exactly what happened. That leaves open the possibility that instead of falling, Sheffield was struck by a blunt object."

Constance shook her head vehemently. This was insane; she couldn't believe it was happening. "The police who came to my apartment found Sheffield lying right beside the marble coffee table. They saw the glasses on the floor, the wet spot on the rug, everything. How could anyone seriously doubt what happened?"

"I'll be straight with you," Flynn said. "If Sheffield was Joe Schmoe from Peoria, they'd stamp this one Case Closed and be done with it. But the media, the Sheffield family and a whole lot of other important people are breathing down Morgenstern's neck.

He's almost got to do something or risk being hung out to dry in the next election.''

"Which means what?'' Constance asked. She swallowed hard and forced herself to say the words she had been avoiding ever since the whole horrible mess began. "Is he going to arrest me?''

Flynn shook his head. "That would be grossly premature under the circumstances. Ben knows I'd rake him over the coals for it. What he *has* done is ask for two things. He wanted to know your whereabouts, which I told him because there was no good reason not to. Our main concern is to keep you from the media, and Ben won't leak anything to them, that's not how he works. The second thing he wants is permission to search your apartment. I advise you to grant it because if you don't, he'll just get a warrant. Being cooperative at this point can only strengthen our case.''

Despite herself Constance felt a surge of resentment. She hated the sense that her life was slipping beyond her control. Sheffield's invasion of her privacy and her safety seemed to go on and on.

"I don't get this,'' she said. "I didn't do anything wrong, so why am I being made to feel as though I did?''

Flynn looked at her over the bridge of his fingers. "You know the answer to that as well as I do. We all like to think that justice is blind, but that just isn't true. The Sheffield family has clout. They're using it.''

"But Lewis is *dead*. Why can't they let him rest? Why go on pretending he was something that he wasn't?''

"You'd have to ask them that,'' Flynn said. "If he was habitually violent and abusive toward women, maybe they just can't admit it to themselves even now. Tonight I'm scheduled to attend a social event where Charles Sheffield is likely to be present. I want you to come along. I think it would be useful for him to get a direct look at you and for us to see how he reacts."

Constance paled. The thought of having to confront the brother of the man who had tried to rape her and who was dead as a result was almost more than she could contemplate. But then she considered her own sense of helplessness and violation, and how that was still continuing because of the Sheffield family's misuse of their power. Pride demanded that she not give in to them.

"All right," she said, "I'll go."

"Good. What about Morgenstern and your apartment?"

She hesitated. Flynn's advice was solid, but the pill was still hard to swallow. "Tell him to go ahead," she said finally. "I have nothing to hide."

A gleam of satisfaction shone in his amber eyes. He looked like a man who had bet heavily and saw the odds shifting in his favor. He had said he believed her but the belief wasn't unshakable. Until they came up with a solid explanation for Sheffield's attack on her, Flynn would keep testing, questioning and probing. He wouldn't be able to let it rest. Constance was just beginning to realize that neither would she. Like it or not, they had become partners in the search for an elusive treasure called truth.

She left his office a short time later and decided to walk back to Dominique's. On the way she stopped in a small shop she knew and bought a dress to wear that evening. Flynn had indicated the event was a charity

ball and strictly formal. There were several dresses in
her closet that would have done the job, but he didn't
want her returning to her apartment until after the
police had searched it. It was vital, he explained, to
avoid even the appearance of trying to conceal evidence.

Constance reminded herself of that as she dug out
her credit card and handed it over. Whatever else was
going on in her life, her wardrobe was certainly bene-
fiting. There was the old silver-lining argument again,
which took her back to her comment the previous
evening about not being interested in Flynn as a man.
It hadn't been true then and it sure wasn't now. She
shook her head wryly. In the worse trouble of her life,
up to her neck in problems, and she picked now to
meet a man who made her feel things she never had
before. As dyed-in-the-wool New Yorkers would say,
go figure.

She got back to the hotel with barely an hour to
spare before Flynn was due. In a rush she showered,
shampooed and dressed. Right on time the bedside
phone pealed.

This time there was no mistake about it; the women
in the lobby were definitely staring at him. Constance
couldn't blame them. In a business suit he looked
fantastic. In evening clothes he was downright lethal.
The light gleaming off his hair gave it a silvery sheen.
His skin was burnished, his posture erect. He looked
tough, confident and unapologetically masculine.

The previous evening she had worn black. It had
suited her mood, and besides, you couldn't go wrong
with it. But a change of pace had been called for if she
was going to face the Sheffields. The gown she'd cho-

sen was blue, the same azure shade as her eyes. In deference to the still-chilly evenings, it was a knit with a turtleneck collar and long sleeves. When she moved, it clung to her, outlining the high, full curve of her breasts, her slim waist and the tapered smoothness of her hips. She wore it without jewelry, with a minimum of makeup and with her hair down. She knew the look suited her and her mood reflected that. She felt calmer than she had before and a good deal more assured. Which was just as well, she thought, as she met Flynn's eyes. For a second there he looked just a bit ruffled.

In fact, he felt as though he'd been slammed in the solar plexus. Every time he saw her, she was more beautiful, more desirable, more evocative of everything he had ever wanted in a woman. It was taking all his willpower to remember that their relationship was, and had to remain, purely professional.

Still, he couldn't prevent himself from saying what was uppermost in his mind. "You look very beautiful."

Constance felt the warmth creeping over her cheeks. Other men had told her the same thing, but coming from Flynn, it actually meant something. "Thank you," she murmured. A moment of awkwardness descended on them both before Flynn broke it. He reached out his hand, took hers gently and led her from the hotel.

Chapter 5

The Metropolitan Museum of Art is a sprawling, nineteenth-century building located in the seventies along Fifth Avenue. It backs up into Central Park, with its entrance facing a row of apartment houses that are home to an international cast of the rich and famous. During the day the museum and its vast collection are host to schoolchildren, senior citizens groups, tourists and even a few city dwellers who wander in more or less by accident. But at night the character of the place changes. It becomes the site of invitation-only parties where a lucky few hundred are wined and dined amid much of the world's great art.

Constance knew all this as she climbed the wide marble stairs to the main entrance. She had been to several such functions given by large corporations for which her agency worked. But she had never been to anything that approached the level of the party being thrown by the newly formed Society for the Renewal and Reclamation of Yohuba—SORRY.

Yohuba, for the uninitiated, was a small, picturesque island in the South Pacific, home to half a thousand happy citizens until being decimated by a toxic-waste spill from a passing tanker. The discovery that the tanker's cargo had included lethal chemicals from virtually every industrialized country, all anxious to dispose of them far from their own shores, had roused public ire. Overnight little Yohuba became the symbol of Paradise Lost and the focus of well-intentioned efforts from a vast range of sources including SORRY.

Several Yohuban citizens were on hand in the large Temple Court of the museum to lend a note of solemnity to the proceedings. They looked not at all surprised by the glittering array of New York's most fashionable, nor by the blaring music, flowing drink and exotic foods carried on silver trays and hoisted by out-of-work actors. Later one of the Yohubans would be quoted as saying that the event reminded him of certain burial rites common among his people, which in turn set off a wave of interest in Yohuban culture culminating in the founding of a School of Yohuban Studies at Yale University—SYSYU.

The Yohubans aside, most of those present were members of the city's financial and political elite. The usual crowd that came out for such occasions to show off and sniff out or otherwise scarf up anything that might be of interest or, in other words, profitable. Most were older men with younger women, the so-called trophy wives who were the walking, talking equivalent of hundred-foot yachts with the advantage of being more easily maneuverable and, depending on the current price of oil, possibly less expensive to maintain.

Beside such women, whose most intimate relationships were with their plastic surgeons and personal fitness trainers, Constance felt as close to dowdy as she could come until she remembered the look in Flynn's eyes when he'd seen her. Her shoulders straightened and she smiled slightly as they stepped into the throng.

That was Charles Sheffield's first impression of her—a beautiful, confident woman on the arm of one of the most powerful and respected defense attorneys in the country. He broke off his conversation with an ambitious city council member—were there any other kind?—and stared at her.

Flynn spotted him across the room but said nothing to Constance. He knew Charles Sheffield by reputation and through a few chance encounters at occasions such as this one. Everyone agreed he was a brilliant manipulator of money and people, although there was disagreement about how much of that was Sheffield himself and how much was the influence of his mother. Whatever the truth of the matter, Flynn found him cold and not particularly intelligent outside his narrow field of expertise.

Briefly he ran over in his mind what he knew about the elder and only remaining Sheffield son. Charles was in his late thirties, five years older than his dead brother. Unlike Lewis he was married with three children. Also unlike Lewis, he had a picture-perfect record of the right schools, the right organizations, the right jobs and so on. If the man had ever veered from the straight and narrow, no one knew it. A shade over six feet with blond hair and gray eyes, he looked like most people's idea of a youngish British aristocrat. Flynn suspected the image was carefully crafted and disdained the effort. He smiled mirthlessly in Sheffield's direction and was rewarded by a frown.

The exchange did not go unnoticed by others. People moved forward as subtly as they could manage so as not to miss anything. Meanwhile, Constance remained unaware of what was happening. She accepted a drink from a passing waiter, but her attention was focused on the small, gemlike Egyptian temple that dominated that part of the museum. The temple was a gift from a grateful Egyptian government in acknowledgment of the museum's role in saving priceless artifacts. An entire wing of the museum had been constructed around it, creating a spacious court in which the austere beauty of the ancient building appeared almost to gloat before those who came to marvel at it.

Flynn noticed Constance's distraction and was touched by it. Alone among the crowd assembled in the Temple Court, she was actually paying attention to something that reached beyond the here and now. As a member of the New York social scene, she didn't come across too well. As a human being, she got top marks.

She still hadn't noticed anything amiss, but that couldn't last much longer. Rather than have her taken by surprise, Flynn said quietly, "Sheffield's here."

Her hand tightened on his arm. "Where?"

"Over there. The tall guy with the dark blond hair."

To his surprise, and pleasure, Constance did not glance in the direction he indicated. Instead, she kept her attention on the temple and appeared as unruffled as ever.

"Does he know we're here?" she asked.

"Sure does. So does everyone else in the immediate vicinity." He grinned down at her. "Next to money, scandal is the breath of life in this town." Her expression faltered. Gently he added, "Smile, sweetheart, it's show time."

Constance noted the endearment but stored it away for later. She stiffened her shoulders, lifted her head and gave him a look that could only be described as radiant.

"Bravo," a voice said behind them.

She turned to find a small, plump man grandly dressed in a purple jacket and puce neckerchief smiling at them both. The man's soft, round face was familiar to her and just about anyone else who watched television. In his youth he had been a writer of some genius and even more renown. Later he became a celebrity, one of those who popped up on the nightly talk shows, declaiming archly about this and that. There were rumors that he was trying to write again, but it was anyone's guess if they were true or not. Whatever the case, he hadn't lost his curiosity or his inclination to mischief.

"Flynn," he exclaimed, loudly enough to be overheard by their avid audience and enthusiastically enough to create the impression that he and the attorney were long-lost brothers. "How *have* you been? Off slaying dragons again or just making it hot for the district attorney?"

"Nice to see you, too, Howard," Flynn said cordially. "This is Miss Lehane. Constance, meet Howard Bartlett. Don't believe a word he says, just enjoy it.''

"Cruel, cruel," Bartlett intoned as he took Constance's hand and bent over it. "Such a pleasure. Not only are you lovely, but I do so admire people with entertainment value. Now don't think for a moment I'm belittling the whole dreadful experience you're going through—''

"You aren't?" Constance asked mildly. She supposed she should have been annoyed, but Bartlett had been one of her favorite writers in college and she figured he'd earned some tolerance.

"Not at all," he insisted. "It's only that bad times or good, life does have to be gotten through, doesn't it? I've always thought it so much better to try to find a little amusement along the way." He glanced at Flynn. "I suppose this was your idea, wasn't it? It positively smacks of you. Who else would bring this lovely creature directly into the lion's den?''

Flynn spread his hands disarmingly. "Hey, I happen to be a big fan of the Yohubans. I'm just turning out to support them like everyone else."

Bartlett wiggled the prodigious eyebrows that seemed to weigh down his face. "You do know the whole five hundred of them have been transported to Maui, where they're living it up in hotel suites paid for by their devoted admirers? The chief told me a few minutes ago that they're getting very fond of room service and cable TV. Getting them to go home again ain't gonna be easy."

"It never is," Flynn said. "So how's the book going, Bartlett?''

"Slowly, slowly. Life keeps intruding. I'm working on a little piece for—" He named a popular men's magazine. "All about the decline and fall of New York society since the end of the 1980s. Remember how much fun it was back then? Just one long endless hoopla with everyone out to get whatever they could and no regrets. Not like now. Everything's gotten so much more complicated."

Flynn shrugged. "Like you said, that's life. By the way, rumor has it Lewis Sheffield was up to a few things he shouldn't have been. You know anything about that?"

Constance dared a quick glance at Flynn. He looked perfectly matter-of-fact, as though he'd inquired after the weather rather than dropped a live grenade into the middle of the conversation.

Bartlett, however, was under no such misconception. He took a quick step backward and smiled nervously. "Rumor, you say? Never listen to it myself." He glanced over his shoulder as though considering a hasty retreat, but then thought better of it. Like it or not, Flynn was simply too big a catch, at least potentially, to walk away.

The writer dropped his voice to a conspiratorial whisper and leaned closer. "I'd have to be mad to risk getting the Sheffields upset at me. Do let me say just one thing. These are genuinely serious people. Elizabeth Sheffield is a true survivor. She came up out of the most god-awful poverty all the way to the top, and nothing, absolutely nothing, is going to knock her off her perch. She's the proverbial steel hand in the steel glove, and if you know what's good for you, you'll give her a wide berth."

"That isn't really an option, is it?" Flynn observed quietly.

Bartlett looked startled for a moment, as though he had lost track of the situation. The notion of anyone going head-to-head with the Sheffields was so outlandish that he hadn't truly considered it until that moment.

His recovery was agile. "Ah, well, it's all grist for the mill, isn't it? Men and women suffer, struggle, live and die while writers get fat on the proceeds. It does make one wonder about the Almighty's priorities, but never mind. Do keep in touch, dear boy, Miss Lehane. I absolutely must know how all this comes out."

He wandered off with a vague smile. Constance turned to Flynn. "What was all that about?"

"Just Bartlett doing what he does best."

"That used to be writing. What is it now?"

"Stirring the pot. He sent a message—call it the party line—don't mess with the Sheffields. That's not exactly news. But we sent one in return that's liable to ruffle a few feathers, namely that if we're pushed, we'll shatter Lewis Sheffield's reputation so thoroughly all his family's wealth and power won't be enough to put it back together again. There won't be a rock the man crawled under that we'll leave unturned."

"You might as well have declared war," Constance said quietly. She wasn't criticizing him, just stating a fact. They both knew the stakes were too high for anything less.

"The Sheffields did that," Flynn replied, "when they started pressuring Morgenstern. Maybe it sounds naive, but from where I sit, no one does that to the law and walks away scot-free.''

"Don't worry about it," Constance said.

"About what?"

"Being naive. Like I said, the last I heard, it wasn't a crime."

He laughed, meeting her eyes. "And I said it should be," he remembered. "Tough guy."

"That's you. Superlawyer."

He flushed slightly. Her gentle mockery disarmed him. He had the feeling that she was seeing past the public image to the man within. He wasn't used to such perceptiveness. At the same time that it made him uneasy, he couldn't deny the appeal of it. But then Constance herself was a very appealing woman. Maybe afterward, when she was no longer his client, he'd be able to do something about that. If he lasted that long.

"Let's get something to eat," he said.

A buffet was set up along one wall of the Temple Court. Waiters were carving whole hams and haunches of beef, and baskets overflowed with fresh-baked rolls. There were paper-thin slices of salmon and heaps of fruit, platters of cheese and pâtés, a veritable cornucopia of goodies waiting to be sampled.

Constance was unabashedly hungry. If this whole thing went on much longer, she'd have to start a diet, and she absolutely hated the idea of that. (Exercising was fine; she enjoyed that, but dieting stank.)

"Maybe I'll only have one of those," she murmured, eyeing translucent slices of smoked ham wrapped around asparagus.

"Have two," Flynn insisted. "They're good for you."

"Just out of morbid curiosity, how do you figure that?"

"Asparagus is a vegetable, right? Better yet, it's green. My mother always told me to eat those."

"What about the ham?"

"Yeah, well, there's not much to that, is there? What harm could it do?"

"I see your point." She placed two on her plate and ignored the little twinge of guilt. "But that's absolutely it. Let's find a place to sit down."

They located a small table set up near a fountain that provided a rush of cool air in contrast to the increasingly overheated atmosphere. As they took their seats, people at the surrounding tables made a point of taking no notice of them. Constance sighed. Only true celebrities were subject to the full New York treatment intended to demonstrate that everyone here was so cool the Queen of England could have walked in on her hands and nobody would so much as blink. It was all baloney, of course. Every quivering little nerve ending was tuned in their direction. More to the point, so was every ear.

"Lovely evening," Constance said, seeking as nondescript a comment as she could muster.

"Great," Flynn said. "I like that dress, by the way. It compliments your eyes."

Constance stared at him. What on earth had gotten into the man? "Uh ... thanks."

He leaned closer across the table and put his hand over hers. His smile was warmly intimate. "Relax," he murmured. "You're doing great."

The sudden contact of his skin against hers made her flush. His hand was warm, large and callused along the fingers and palm. It wasn't the hand of a man who spent his days shuffling papers, but then the rest of him didn't seem to be that way, either. She swallowed hastily and wondered why she felt no impulse to pull away. A single friendly look from the young man on the bus the previous day had been enough to bring back all her horror and revulsion at what Lewis had attempted. Why didn't she feel anything like that with Flynn? He was far more masculine and potentially intimidating. In a struggle against Lewis, she'd had at least some chance of success. With Flynn she would have none. Yet with him she felt safe and protected, as though some part of her instinctively recognized that he would never hurt her.

That instinctive trust carried her through the bewilderment she felt at his words and actions. She even managed to return his smile. "Is this Act One or Act Two?" she asked.

"Act Two. Act One was the little scene with Bartlett wherein we established my intentions, namely to make things very hot for the Sheffields. We are now giving them a reason why I would do that. Since simple moral outrage doesn't carry much weight with these folks, I decided on something a bit more creative."

Constance nodded slowly. "I see, I think. The idea is to convey the impression that your involvement in this case may go beyond the strictly professional."

"It's called psyching out the opposition."

"It's also called being devious, presumptuous and arrogant as all get-out, and those are the good points."

The businesslike Flynn was attractive enough; this teasing, seductive version was devastating. For a moment she let herself imagine what it would be like to be desired by him. The thought was so enticing that she shied away from it before she could become too deeply enmeshed.

"Have you used this tactic before?" she asked.

Flynn shook his head. He didn't care to examine why he was doing so now. In his younger years he'd been plagued by a certain impulsiveness that sometimes led him into hot water. Gradually he'd learned more self-control, but where Constance was concerned, his hard-won restraint wasn't holding up too well. He suspected that the excuse he'd given of psyching out Ben and the Sheffields was just that, a smoke screen thrown over his own feelings. Still, a little confusion tossed their way wouldn't be a bad thing, especially when he was experiencing so much of it himself.

"What's Act Three?" Constance asked, not certain she wanted to hear the answer.

Flynn met her eyes. His smile was gone. Softly he said, "Act Three is where I take you back to Dominique's, say good-night and go back to the office to get some more work done. I've got a feeling tomorrow's going to be a busy day."

Constance didn't know whether she was relieved or disappointed. She suspected a bit of both. But the strain of being the object of so much interest was beginning to wear on her. She felt the scrutiny of eyes following them as they walked hand-in-hand from the party. In their wake the conversation resumed with heightened urgency. In some ways New York was an amazingly insular city. By tomorrow word would have spread of their appearance together, and people would be speculating on the exact nature of their relationship. It should have dismayed her, since she was an intrinsically private person. Instead, she felt a spurt of amusement at the thought that she wouldn't be alone in her surprise and uncertainty. A whole lot of other people would be sharing it with her.

Maybe they could all get together and offer suggestions. What would a cross section of New Yorkers say about her situation?

"A nice girl like you in a mess like this. That's what comes from not listening to your mother."

"You could'a stayed home—where was it, Ohio?—married a local boy, had a few kids."

"Nice place, Ohio. I think I flew over it once."

"Don' lissen to them, you're better off here. He's an okay guy considerin' he's from Hoboken. He'll pull you through."

"A professional man, handsome, not hurting for money. You got any sense, you grab him."

"Does he have any brothers?"

"Uncles?"

"Cousins?"

"He's not gay, is he?"

"Gay, schmay, he's gorgeous. Look at her, her toes are curling."

"What are you laughing at?" Flynn asked. He was glancing at her with a touch of concern, as if he thought she might be losing it right there on the steps of the museum.

"Nothing," Constance said. "Say, did you ever hear the one about the lawyer who gets to heaven and—"

"Oh, God, the woman knows lawyer jokes. I've got a million of them. Come on, we'll swap on the way."

Ten minutes later they reached the hotel laughing. Flynn insisted on seeing Constance to her room. He did it with such old-world charm that she couldn't resist. Truth be told, she didn't want to. All those strange, unexpected feelings were catching up with her. She felt as though the real world —the one she understood and could predict to at least some degree— didn't count for much at the moment.

They got off the elevator and walked down the carpeted hallway to her door. She fished in her evening bag for the key. Flynn took it from her and turned the lock. He handed the key back gravely.

"Get a good night's rest," he said. His voice was low and husky, and he looked as though what he was saying had nothing whatsoever to do with what he was thinking.

"Flynn—" she murmured. Her eyes were wide and filled with questions. Her lips parted on a soundless breath.

Desire raged through him. It came so hard and fast that it caught him unawares. He thought he'd had it all under control. Say good-night, leave, go home, suffer. Nothing complicated about that. But there it was, that surging primal need that knocked little things like reason right off their perches and left them kicking in the dust, howling uselessly.

Sweet lord, he wanted her! So much that it scared him. She was coming off a brutal encounter. Her life was riddled with uncertainty. If he had any compassion, any class, any brains, he'd slam a lid on his feelings and walk away.

So he didn't have any of those things. So he was simply a man caught in the throes of emotions so powerful he was drowning in them. Way off in the distance, he thought for sure he could hear Mother Nature laughing. Not any polite little chuckle, but the wholehearted belly whoop the lady gave when she caught humans doing just what she expected of them.

So who was he to argue?

He bent his head, blocking out the light from the crystal fixtures along the wall. Shadows fell across them both. Constance stiffened slightly, but she made no effort to pull away. The door was open behind her, she had a clear line of retreat. She just didn't choose to use it.

Choices, that was what it was all about. Sheffield had tried to take them away from her. Flynn literally left the door wide open. She swayed and raised her hands instinctively. They landed against the hard wall of his chest.

The contact sent tremors through them both. He murmured something, her name? She couldn't really be sure because speech was beyond them both. His mouth brushed hers, lightly, sweetly, so tempting that she could not help but respond.

Flynn's arms closed around her. His mouth hardened, becoming demanding. She answered in kind, helpless to do otherwise.

They were lost, engulfed in one another, until abruptly the sound of the elevator doors opening again threw them back into reality. Shakily, Flynn raised his head. He looked down at her.

"Constance, I didn't mean for..."

She laid a finger gently on the lips that had tormented her so delightfully a moment before. "I know. I didn't either."

"I'm sorry. You've been through so much..."

"Don't." She eased away from him, smiling gently. How odd that this big, hard man, so habitually in charge of himself and everything else, should need reassurance from her.

"I'm a grown-up, Flynn. I'm responsible for my own actions. And you—well, let's just say that you're very much a gentleman. If I hadn't wanted you to kiss me, I'm certain you wouldn't have."

He released his breath slowly, only then aware that he'd been holding it. She was right, of course. Coercing a woman in any way was repugnant to him. But she was something else, too. Honest. She didn't pretend she hadn't wanted what had happened as much as he had.

Too bad Lewis Sheffield hadn't appreciated her honesty. Too bad he'd been such a bastard. And too bad he was dead. Flynn wouldn't have minded a chance to go one-on-one with him.

Okay, so it was a little primitive, but he was feeling very possessive. Constance wasn't just his client, and there was no sense pretending otherwise. She was... exhausted, that's what. There were shadows under her eyes he hadn't noticed until just then. He'd been too caught up in other things. She was also very pale. All the passion in the world couldn't disguise that.

With consummate gentleness, he put her from him. His smile was thoroughly male. "Like I said, get some rest."

She shook her head ruefully. "Oh, sure. You, too."

He laughed, he couldn't help it. Neither one of them was in for a very restful night. Yet another strike against the Sheffields, Flynn thought to himself. They were running up one hell of a tally. The time was rapidly approaching when he'd have to even the score.

Chapter 6

"Mr. Morgenstern is on the phone," Helen said. She had poked her head into Flynn's office to convey that news. Her tone and the look on her face, as though she smelled something bad, made it clear that she was acting under protest.

Flynn looked up from the stack of papers he was trying to get through and frowned. "Tell him I went fishing."

She was back a moment later. "He says to tell you unless you want your butt full of hooks, you should talk to him now."

"What a guy. Ben! Did Helen say fishing? Jeez, that woman. You work with them, train them and then what happens? *Ow!* Cut it out. So Ben, how's every little thing?"

"Not as good as they seem to be with you, buddy. I hear you're getting out more these days."

"I always got out plenty, Ben. People just didn't pay as much attention. We missed you last night."

"Yeah, I'll bet. Sheffield was on the phone first thing this morning. He wants you up on charges for conflict of interest, unethical behavior and a bunch of other stuff in the same general vein. What do you suppose got him so hot under the collar?"

"Gee, beats me. All I did was take Constance out for a little supper in a good cause. You know, she's really upset about those Yohubans, but then she's that kind of woman."

"You should know. Listen, buddy, this isn't like you. You've always been a tough son of a gun but you never played games before."

"What makes you think I'm doing that now?"

"Come on, you just met the woman. She comes waltzing into your office and cries on your shoulder, and the next thing you're not just representing her, you're taking her out. What gives?"

"You tell me. You're a whole lot better informed about the matter than I am."

Ben sighed. The sound wafted down the telephone line like the exhalation of a great marine mammal—a killer whale, maybe.

"Okay, but one of these days it's gonna be pay-back time. We did the apartment search yesterday evening. By the way, getting her agreement was a smart move."

"What did you find?"

"Nothing. And I do mean *nothing*. No drugs, no dirty movies, no incriminating letters and no trace of the deceased on the marble coffee table that supposedly killed him. Nothing."

"Did the autopsy show an external injury?"

"No," the D.A. admitted, "the wound was internal. But we could have found a few scraps of hair on the table corner, something to show what she says happened actually did. Instead, it was clean as a whistle."

"You know as well as I do that he could have hit that table a glancing blow as he fell and there would have been no trace of it. You're grasping at straws, Ben."

"Maybe, maybe not. But I've had two city council members, a retired judge and a Nobel Prize winner for God's sake call me up since yesterday to tell me what a fantastic guy Lewis Sheffield was. Salt of the earth, Rock of Gibraltar, the whole nine yards. I'm telling you, Flynn, by the time I got off the phone I was close to tears. If these people are to be believed, the world's lost a saint."

"What does that tell you, Ben?"

"That my neck's in a wringer, which I definitely do not like. Find me something, Flynn. Anything that explains why Lewis Sheffield would do what your client says he did. You come up with a plausible explanation, she's off the hook. Otherwise, I've got no choice but to go to the grand jury."

"I hear you but I need some time. Also more information, a copy of the autopsy to start with."

"A week, tops, and I'll get you the info, but that's the best I can do. And by the way, we haven't talked."

Flynn hung up the phone and stared at it for a few moments before he abruptly swung his chair around and stood up. Helen had discreetly absented herself from the office while he was talking.

"Morgenstern's sending over a file," Flynn said as he headed out of his office. "Make sure nobody else gets a hold of it."

"Where are you going?" she called after him.

He strode down the hall, pulling on his suit jacket as he went. Over his shoulder he said, "Fishing."

Constance sat on the bed in her room and stared at the phone for several minutes before deciding what she had to do. Ever since her conversation with Flynn at La Sylphide, she'd been thinking about calling home. Putting it off hadn't made the task any easier.

Abruptly she reached for the receiver, punched in the number and waited while the call went through. Her mother answered almost at once. Constance could picture her in the kitchen of the big white house that overlooked the town's college campus and the river beyond.

"Hi," she said cheerily. "It's me. How're you doing?"

"Fine," her mother replied. If she was surprised at hearing from her daughter unexpectedly, she didn't reveal it. "I'm baking angel food cakes for the church sale this weekend. How are things in the big city?"

"Pretty much as usual. Listen, Mom, there's something I need to tell you about. I wanted you and Dad to hear it from me rather than someone else."

"What's wrong?" her mother asked. She didn't sound frightened or worried, but all her attention was clearly focused on her daughter. Mary Lehane had lived all her life in a small midwestern town, a life that by any measure had been sheltered and without great challenges. Yet she possessed a courage and resilience her daughter couldn't help but envy.

"A man I knew had an accident in my apartment and died. Some people, particularly his family, are trying to suggest that I was responsible. That isn't true, but just to be on the safe side, I've gotten a good lawyer. It should all be taken care of very soon, but in the meantime I wanted you to know so you wouldn't worry if you heard things from other people."

"What kind of accident?" Mary asked.

"He slipped and hit his head on a corner of the coffee table."

"The marble one?" Her mother had complimented her on the table when she and Constance's father had visited New York a couple of years before.

"That's right."

"How terrible for you. I hope you're not staying there alone now?"

"No, actually I'm staying in a hotel for a while." She gave her mother the name and phone number and waited while she wrote them down. "Like I said, I've gotten a good lawyer and I'm sure this will all be taken care of quickly."

"Why does his family think you could be responsible? If it was a simple accident, surely they would realize you couldn't possibly have—"

"It wasn't exactly simple, Mom." This was the part Constance was dreading, but having come so far she felt she had to go on. "The man's name was Lewis Sheffield. When he asked me to have dinner with him, he seemed like a perfectly nice person. But when we got back to my apartment he turned very aggressive.

We ended up struggling. Some drinks were spilled, he slipped on the wet rug and the rest I've told you.''

Mary Lehane was silent for a moment before she said flatly, ''He tried to rape you.''

''I didn't say... How did you know that?''

''The same thing happened to Augusta Sterling's daughter when she went away to college. It was awful. She went to the school administration for help but she got the feeling no one believed her.''

''I know the feeling,'' Constance said grimly. ''What happened to her?''

''She transferred to another school and seems to be back on track now, just a whole lot more careful. As for the young man, nothing at all happened to him. He's free to try it again anytime he likes.''

''That isn't the case here. Lewis Sheffield is dead, and his family is trying to blame me for it. But don't worry, they won't get away with it. I just don't want you and Dad surprised by anything you may read or hear.''

''Sweetheart,'' her mother said gently, ''we know you couldn't possibly be to blame and we'll make that clear to anyone who suggests otherwise. Don't give us another thought. It's you who matters. Do you want us to come out?''

''No,'' Constance said quietly. She was deeply touched by the offer. Without doubt her parents would stand shoulder-to-shoulder with her, come what may. At an earlier time in her life she wouldn't have hesitated to accept their help. But she was older now and far better able to rely on herself, thanks in no small part to everything they had done to raise her.

"Thank you," she went on. "I really appreciate it but I'm convinced this will all be settled soon." Deliberately she switched the conversation to more pleasant topics, inquiring after her sister's children and the vegetable garden her mother put in every year. Mary Lehane accepted the diversion, but as they were preparing to hang up she said, "Just remember we're here whenever you need us. We love you very much."

"I love you, too, Mom," Constance said quietly. She blinked hard as she put down the phone. Flynn had been right; she had needed to touch base with home. The solidness there and the unconditional love were a balm to her troubled spirit. She went into the bathroom and splashed cold water on her face, looking at herself in the mirror. Mary Lehane's daughter wasn't going to let anyone turn her into a victim, not Lewis Sheffield and not his family. If they wanted a fight, they were going to get it.

Flynn had said the next step was to start finding people who had known Lewis and might be willing to talk about him. Constance knew just where to start.

Dominique was in her office behind the reception desk. "Come in," she said when she saw Constance at the door. "I was just thinking about you. Did you enjoy last night's little soiree?"

"Was I supposed to?" Constance replied with a smile. She took the seat Dominique indicated on the couch beside her. The older woman was perfectly groomed as always, in a Carl Legerfeld suit with her ebony-and-silver hair gathered in a chignon. She had been working and had a little pair of tortoiseshell glasses perched on her nose. As she removed them and placed them neatly on the small table in front of her,

Constance couldn't help but notice that her eyes were bright with amusement.

"I suppose you've heard all about it," she said.

Dominique nodded. "News that interesting spreads fast. It seems as though you and Flynn made quite an impression. How is the dear man, by the way?"

"In rare form even for him. I get the feeling he's breaking rules right and left."

"Your instincts are good. I've never known him to be seen socially with a client before." Dominique paused. "Howard Bartlett has been regaling everyone with the details on his conversation with you and Flynn. He does go on a bit, but one can always count on Howard for a good story."

"Is there any chance that his story's also accurate?" Constance asked.

"I don't know. Is it true that you and Flynn 'positively radiated erotic synergy'?"

Constance's eyebrows shot up. "Gee, I don't think so. What's synergy, anyway?"

"Cooperative action particularly in the performance of complex body movements."

"We were standing still at the time."

"Howard does tend to exaggerate. At any rate, I do believe Flynn made his point. Now, what can I do for you?"

"You can tell me where to start tracking down Lewis Sheffield's friends, people outside of the family who knew him well and would be willing to talk about him."

It was Dominique's turn to look startled. "Why do you want to do that?"

"Because there has to be somebody out there who knew the real man, not the plaster saint his family is trying to concoct. I need to find that person or persons if I'm going to have any chance of proving that I'm telling the truth."

"You shouldn't have to prove it," Dominique said softly. "That isn't how our legal system is supposed to work."

"Tell that to Ben Morgenstern and the Sheffield family. I've researched Lewis's background, I know where he went to school, where he worked and so on. But I have no sense of who he really was or why he did what he did. Until I can remedy that, there's a very real danger that the family will convince the D.A. to proceed against me."

"I see," Dominique said quietly. "You must realize that people will be very reluctant to tell you anything the Sheffields wouldn't want you to hear?"

"Of course, but I still have to try."

"Also, word of what you're doing is bound to get back to the family. That will only make them angrier."

"Let it. I refuse to knuckle under to these people. Whatever happens, I simply can't live like that."

Dominique looked at her assessingly. "What does Flynn have to say about all this?"

"He's all for it, only I'm afraid he'll try to do it himself without my being very involved. But I need to actively defend myself. It's hard to explain exactly but—"

"No, it isn't," Dominique broke in. "You need to reclaim control of your own life, not simply have Flynn give it back to you. That makes perfect sense."

She was silent for a moment before she said, "I can give you a few names but not very much. Lewis Sheffield tended to keep a fairly low profile."

"I wonder why. He wasn't a particularly modest or humble man."

"He may have simply been bored by the social scene or been too busy with his filmmaking. Don't try to read too much into anything before you're sure of what you've got." She paused a moment before she asked, "I suppose you're already aware of Delia Russell?"

"I wasn't when I accepted Lewis's invitation to dinner, but I am now. Were they really going to be married?"

"That isn't clear. Certainly they were never formally engaged. At any rate, there are other people who could be more helpful." She rattled off several names as Constance listened intently. When she was done, she said, "I'm afraid that's the best I can do. As I mentioned, Lewis Sheffield wasn't the most public of men. If you wanted information on his brother, for instance, that would be a different story. But under the circumstances..."

"What about his mother?" Constance asked.

Dominique's eyes widened slightly in alarm. "You're not thinking of going to see her?"

"She's not at the top of my list," Constance admitted, "but I would like to know more about her. Can you tell me anything?"

Dominique sighed. "Elizabeth Sheffield is a fascinating woman. She exudes the kind of allure common to all beautiful, dangerous things. I suppose she's in her midseventies now if she's a day, but in her youth she was absolutely breathtaking. She captivated New York society, which is saying something considering how cynical and world-weary this town can get. More to the point, she captivated Phillip Sheffield. He was considerably older, about twenty years, I think, and he'd been married twice before. I suppose you'd call him a playboy, at least until he met Elizabeth. They had one of those relationships in which two people are completely wrapped up in each other to the exclusion of virtually everyone else."

"Including their children?" Constance asked softly.

"Oh, yes, I'd say so. That sort of thing isn't uncommon among their social class. I imagine no one thought much of it. Charles went off to school very early, he was eight, I believe. With Lewis they waited awhile longer but then off he went, too. There was great emphasis on toughening up, being a man and so on. You know," she said thoughtfully, "people imagine that children of very wealthy families have wonderful lives, but in fact they can be dreadfully barren. I can't remember who said it but somebody has pointed out that rich families and poor ones can share many of the same characteristics—a tendency toward too much drinking, drugs, divorces or outright abandonment, that sort of thing. Money is no guarantee of happiness or even moderate contentment."

"It certainly doesn't seem to have been for the Sheffields," Constance said. "Is there anything else you can tell me about Elizabeth?"

"Only that if I were you, I'd be careful of her. She's hard as nails."

"Howard Bartlett said pretty much the same thing."

"You should listen to him. Heaven knows, his mind's not what it used to be, but he still has enough sense to be cautious of people like the Sheffields."

"Are there others like them? I'm getting the impression they're in a class by themselves."

Dominique nodded. "You may be right. Certainly there are other powerful, wealthy families that care tremendously about their image, but the Sheffields go rather further than that. They simply hate to be thwarted in any way. My guess is that Elizabeth Sheffield had plans for her younger son. He may have been resisting them but eventually he would have fallen in line. Now he can't."

"What kind of plans, do you have any idea?"

Dominique shrugged. "This business with Delia Russell, she was very young and Lewis never showed any interest in that type before. An alliance between the Russells and Sheffields could have had many benefits for them both. At any rate, my point is that you must do what you think right, but do it cautiously."

Constance remembered those words a short time later as she left the hotel. There was a part of her that would have liked to confront Elizabeth Sheffield directly and without delay. Or to tackle Delia Russell headlong. But common sense held her back.

Even if there was something to gain in any such encounters, what would she say to either woman? When she came right down to it, she knew very little about Lewis Sheffield, even to the point of not knowing *what* questions to ask about him. She needed to remedy that ignorance and to do it fast.

And the most likely place to start seemed to be at the beginning, the place where she and Sheffield first met.

Chapter 7

The studios of Stellar Pictures were located in Long Island City, directly across the East River from Manhattan. Although the two areas were only minutes apart by mass transit, they might as well have been separated by thousands of miles.

Manhattan was L.I.C.'s rich, svelte sister—fur coats versus cloth, legs tanned on the Riviera versus support hose and four inches taller and thirty pounds lighter, married to the guy who was going to make president of his corporation before forty, while poor old L.I.C. had to be glad her husband had a union job that paid enough to feed the kids.

Except for one little thing: recently L.I.C. had gone on a diet and dropped the extra pounds, bought herself a new wardrobe and on her way home from aerobics one day taken a chance on what turned out to be the winning lottery ticket. In other words, the place had turned a corner. Folks who couldn't afford Manhattan rents anymore, or who had just gotten tired of being royally ripped off, had discovered it. They were busy renovating the old buildings into apartments and offices.

Long, long ago—back in the days of silent films— there had been movie studios in Long Island City. Now there were again. Stellar, for one, was located in a sprawling warehouse just within sight of the river.

Constance had been there several times before as part of her work on the Stellar account. She paid off the cabbie and climbed the few steps to the main entrance. The outside of the building was drab and nondescript, but once inside the atmosphere changed drastically.

The reception area was painted in shades of red and black, and the floor repeated the same colors in tiny tiles that curved and flowed back on each other with dizzying effect. The furnishings were all free-form plastic chairs, with couches and tables in the same hues so that they appeared to blend into the walls and floor. Even the receptionist seemed to be camouflaged in red-and-black overalls. Had it not been for her spiked hair, dyed a cheerful purple, and the constant motion of her jaw as she chewed gum, she might have been indistinguishable from her surroundings.

"Yeah?" she said by way of greeting. She was new since Constance's last visit and did not recognize Constance. Nor did she show any particular curiosity as to who she might be. Her attention was on the demanding job of placing kitten stickers on each of her long, lacquered nails. Interruptions made the task all the harder and were definitely not welcome.

"Don't get up," Constance said hastily, ignoring the obvious fact that she would never have considered doing so. "I know where I'm going. Sorry to bother you."

The girl looked puzzled for a moment. Her gum cracked more sharply before she dismissed the errant thought that something might be not quite right. "That's okay."

Constance smiled brightly and pushed past the door that led to a hallway bordered on both sides by offices and conference rooms. Several of the offices were inhabited, but their occupants were nowhere to be seen. At the end of the corridor was the sound stage, an area large enough to hold at least one full-sized airplane. It was crowded with microphones, cameras, lights and scenery in various stages of assembly or disassembly.

Sheffield had been working on a film shortly before his death, but the actual shooting had wrapped up several weeks before. When the sound stage was in operation, several dozen people could be running around there, shouting at each other with various degrees of excitement and desperation. At the moment it was deserted.

But not entirely. Above the sound stage, overlooking it from a height of about twenty feet, was a screening room. It had a large plate-glass window that afforded a view of the action below. When screenings were in progress, venetian blinds were closed to shut out any disturbance.

Looking up, Constance saw that the blinds were shut. In the silence of the empty sound stage, she could hear muted voices and the low throb of music.

She climbed the metal steps to the screening room door and opened it cautiously. In the darkness lit only by the reflected light from the screen, she could make out half a dozen rows of upholstered seats. In one of them, a man sat. The rest were empty. The sound level increased suddenly, drawing her attention to the screen just in time to see a woman's head explode.

She gasped loudly enough to be heard. The man turned around. In the pale red-hued light his features were unrelentingly harsh.

"What're you doing here?" Flynn demanded.

Constance let out a long breath. She forced herself to ignore what was going on up on the screen and walked toward him. "The same thing I suppose you are."

He stood up and met her halfway. "You should have called me first. It's not a good idea for you to be wandering around on your own like this."

"Maybe I did call."

"No, you didn't, I can tell." He took her arm. "Come on, let's go."

"Wait a minute, what about the movie?"

"It stinks."

"So what, it might still tell us something."

"It tells us that Lewis Sheffield had the artistic sensibility of your average nine-year-old. He liked loud noises, bright colors and lots of gore. Maybe that's how he really was and maybe he was just catering to the market, who knows? But you've seen one movie like this, you've seen them all."

The woman on the screen was dead, and another was screaming somewhere off on the side. Constanc shuddered. "There seems to be a bit more to it than that. Are all the victims women?"

"Nice try, but I'm afraid not. Sheffield was a real equal opportunity employer. Everybody—men, women, black, white, whatever—gets it in this thing."

"His other movies weren't like that," Constance said as they left the screening room. "They were violent but they also had other qualities."

"Maybe this one does, too," Flynn replied. "But I'm not sticking around to find out." He let her out of the room as he said, "If Sheffield was revealing anything about himself in his movies, he had it buried under so much trickery and contrivance that it's impossible to find."

Standing on the landing at the top of the stairs, Constance said, "The critics didn't see it that way. They loved his stuff."

Flynn shrugged. "So what? The critics have to love something, most of them can't make a living panning everything. They like to jump on bandwagons, especially if it's one they've helped created. They'll proclaim some guy's a genius just to generate the kind of excitement that makes people pay attention to them."

"That seems a little harsh," Constance said as they went down the steps. "Some of them have studied moviemaking or writing, or whatever for years. They put a lot of thought into what they do."

"A few," Flynn admitted. "But if they're that smart, why aren't they doing what they've studied instead of just critiquing other people's work?"

"I don't know exactly, but not everybody can afford to make movies even if they want to. Lewis Sheffield was a very wealthy man."

"No, actually he wasn't."

Constance stared at him. They were standing at the bottom of the stairs. In the empty silence of the sound stage, her voice sounded unnaturally loud. "What are you talking about?"

"I checked with a banker friend of mine before I came here. The Sheffield money seems to be heavily tied up in various trusts. Some of them were in Lewis's name, but there were a lot of restrictions that in effect prevented him from getting access to anything other than the interest earned on the principal. Do you understand what that means?"

"He could use the new money made by the old money but he couldn't actually do anything with the old money itself."

"Got it. In other words, he was a man on a short leash. The studio and everything in it were heavily mortgaged. His movies had to start making money soon in order for him to avoid going bankrupt. Now it looks as though that will happen anyway."

"I had no idea of that," Constance said softly.

"Too bad. If we could say you knew all about his financial problems and therefore couldn't possibly have been interested in his money, we'd be in better shape."

Her eyes widened. She looked at him in dismay. "Who says I was interested in the money?"

"Nobody, but my bet is that's going to change. So far, the family's whole thrust has been that Lewis was basically a saint and therefore couldn't possibly have done what you say he did. The next step has to be for them to paint him not merely as the innocent party but as the actual victim. It's just a guess, but I think they' say that he was trying to dump you, that you saw all that money going bye-bye, freaked, and killed him. To do that, they have to attack you directly.''

"That's insane," Constance protested. Her stomach clenched. She took a deep breath. "It doesn't matter what they say about me. I can take it."

Flynn shot her a quick look. "Maybe. Anyway, there are at least some people on your side."

Her eyes brightened. "Like who?"

"Come on, I'll introduce you. They're the ones who let me in here."

Behind the sound stage, squirreled away in a corner of the building all its own, was the lunchroom. It was a small space with windows overlooking an air shaft. One wall was taken up with various vending machines whose most nutritious food item was chocolate-covered raisins. A few rickety chairs and tables were spaced across the peeling linoleum floor. Under a tattered sign that said Thank You For Not Smoking was an overflowing ashtray.

Two people sat at a table near the door. They were both young, dressed in jeans and oversize shirts, both with long brown ponytails.

One was a girl. She looked up at Constance and smiled as Flynn introduced them. "Hi, I'm Carrie. It's nice to meet you."

The other was a boy. He nodded somberly. "Hi, I'm Tod. Likewise."

Flynn held out a chair at the table for Constance, then took one for himself. "Carrie and Tod worked for Lewis."

"Slaved for him, you mean," the boy said. He needed no encouragement to talk. The words came in a rush. "There's people saying the guy was a genius. He sure was—at taking advantage of people."

Tod's hands shook slightly as he fumbled for a cigarette. The pack was empty. Flynn took one from his pocket and slid it across the table.

"Can you be more specific?" he asked quietly. "For instance, where did you meet Lewis? How long did you know him?"

"We met out in Berkeley," Carrie said, "a couple of years ago. Tod and I were kind of bumming around, taking a few film courses but not doing much of anything else. Lewis offered us jobs if we'd come east with him."

"At first it was great," Tod said grudgingly. He took a long drag on the cigarette, coughed and added, "We got to do everything we'd only heard about at school. Punching up scripts, running the cameras, editing, even makeup, you name it, we did it. The only problem was that after a while it got to be a real grind. We were working twelve, fourteen hours a day for minimal money, and Lewis didn't always come through with even that. We couldn't afford an apartment; we ended up having to sleep here."

"When the first film came out," Carrie said, "we asked Lewis for more money. He told us to quit if we didn't like the way things were."

"Quit and do what?" Tod put in. "Neither one of us stayed around school long enough to get any kind of degree, and Lewis made sure we didn't share credit on the movies. Where were we supposed to go?"

"Aren't there union regulations against this kind of thing?" Constance asked.

"Of course there are," Carrie said, "but Lewis never paid any attention to them. He figured the studio was small enough that no one would notice, and so far no one has."

Flynn looked from one to the other. "So Sheffield was an unfair employer. Anything else? Did you ever see him get violent, for example?"

They exchanged a glance before Tod said, "Once. Some guy came by who was supposed to be distributing one of the movies, only he wasn't really doing the job and Lewis kind of blew his cork. He grabbed him and pushed him up against the wall outside. Told him that if he didn't cancel the deal right away so Lewis could go to a different distributor, he'd kill him."

"He actually said that," Flynn asked, "that he'd kill him?"

Carrie nodded. "I heard it, too."

"Did you think he was serious?"

She hesitated. "It's hard to say. You know how people make threats sometimes when they're mad, even though they'd never really do anything."

"Was that the only incidence of violence you saw?" Flynn asked.

"There was the time he punched his fists into one of the vending machines," Tod said. He smiled faintly. "The company charged him eight hundred dollars for the damage, and his hand was in a cast for a month."

"What about other kinds of problems?" Flynn went on. He looked at Carrie. "Did you ever experience any kind of harassment from him?"

She hesitated. "What do you mean, harassment?"

"Did he come on to you, try to get you to sleep with m, anything like that?"

She flushed and shook her head. "I wasn't exactly his type; he liked women who were a whole lot more glamorous." She cast a swift glance at Constance. "Besides, he always knew Tod and I were together."

"What are you going to do now?" Constance asked gently. Despite her disappointment that the pair hadn't had anything more concrete to say, she felt sorry for them. They'd gotten a bad deal from Lewis.

"Head back to the coast," Tod said. "When you get down to it, it's the only place to be."

"How are you going to get there?" Flynn asked.

Tod looked surprised. "By plane. We could hitch but it's kind of a drag, and besides, it's not as safe as it used to be."

"I thought you were broke," Constance said.

"We were," Carrie replied. "But this morning Lewis's brother, the older one, came by. He gave us all our back pay plus some extra. He also told us not to talk to anyone about Lewis."

"That guy's a real snot," Tod said. He ground the cigarette out and reached into the pack for another. "He was looking down his nose at us, treating us like we were a couple of tramps. So when you showed up—" he looked at Flynn "—we said, what the hell, why not?"

"I appreciate it," Flynn said gravely. He rose to go, holding out his hand to Tod. "Thanks a lot. Here's my card. If you think of anything else, give me a call."

Tod looked at the card and gave it to Carrie, who put it away carefully in the depths of a cavernous tapestry bag.

"I hope everything works out for you, Mis Lehane," she said softly.

They thanked the pair again and left. Outside in the sunshine Flynn said, "It wasn't much, but it's a start."

"What about what they saw?" Constance asked as they started walking down the street. There were no cabs in sight, but that didn't faze Flynn. He headed for the nearest subway station.

"What about it? Lewis takes out after some guy who's screwing him on distribution. He's a hard-pressed businessman letting off a little steam. There's nothing strange about that. The same with the vending machine. Who among us hasn't been tempted to put a fist through one of those things at some time or another?"

"If it's that meaningless how come you at least think it's a start?"

"Because it's the first crack we've had in the saint-hood story. Lewis Sheffield was a manipulative man who may have been veering toward desperation at least so far as keeping his business going was concerned. We ought to be able to build on that."

"What if we can't?" Constance asked. He was walking so fast that she almost had to run to keep up with him. "What if Tod and Carrie are the best we get?"

"Then we've got a big problem. Put them in front of a grand jury, and you're looking at zero credibility. They'll come across as just a couple of down-in-the-mouth kids with a grudge against their dead boss."

"Slow down," Constance said. She was starting to reathe hard. "Don't you ever just walk?"

"Sorry," Flynn said as he moderated his pace.

They reached the entrance to the subway. Constance hesitated. "I haven't been in one of these in years."

"You're kidding? I use them all the time. The firm gives me a car and driver, but there are parts of the day when you're guaranteed to get stuck in traffic. I can't stand that, so I use the subways instead."

"You really think they're safe?"

"Mostly. They're sure a lot cleaner than they used to be and they run on time."

"About that 'mostly'—"

"I don't think you really have to worry. Most thugs won't bother a guy my size. Besides, I carry a gun."

"You *what?*" Gun permits were almost impossible to get in the City of New York. Only people who could prove demonstrated need were even considered for them.

"It's not a big deal," Flynn said, taking her elbow. He shepherded her gently down the steps. "I've had it for years."

"How did you get it? I mean what reason did you give?"

"A while back I was representing a guy who was being framed for a mob killing. When he walked, I got a few death threats. A cop friend of mine suggested getting the gun. He put the word out on the street that I was armed, and that was the end of the matter."

"Does that kind of thing happen to you often?" Constance asked.

"No, but I deal with a pretty broad range of people. I figure it's always a good idea to be prepared."

He dropped a token in the turnstile and waited while Constance went through before following.

"Is that why you had the cigarettes?" she asked as he joined her on the platform.

He nodded. "You're pretty observant. I haven't smoked in years but I keep stuff like that on hand for situations like the one you just saw. Sometimes a little thing like that can help break the ice."

"It must have worked. Tod was only too happy to talk with you, and the same for Carrie."

"Those two just wanted a little sympathy—and a little respect. My job was basically done for me before I ever walked in there. Charles Sheffield saw to that."

"Did you know he'd been there?" she asked. A train was approaching down the tunnel. She had to raise her voice to be heard above it.

Flynn shook his head. "That was just dumb luck."

"You shouldn't have told me that," she said as the train screeched to a stop and the doors opened. "You could have let me think it was brilliant lawyering."

"Would you have really?" he asked as they stepped inside.

"No, but you could have tried."

Flynn laughed, drawing the wary attention of several people in the car. "I'm not getting away with very much so far, am I?"

"Oh, I don't know about that," Constance said under her breath. Just being close to him was making her heart race a little. The man was so damn attractive. He could have just stood around looking picturesque but oh, no, he had to have a personality and a brain besides.

The train lurched forward, picking up speed. She shifted slightly in her seat and stared out at the black walls of the tunnel racing by. The speed and the darkness combined to give her a sense of things spiraling out of control. It wasn't true, of course, but the feeling was there nonetheless.

She shut her eyes but that didn't help; nothing did. Like it or not, she was on this ride to the end.

Chapter 8

"Where to now?" Constance asked. They were leaving the subway on the Manhattan side. Above-ground the streets were crowded with people hurrying to and from lunch. She glanced around for a moment, envying them the normality of their routine.

"To your apartment," Flynn said.

Constance's attention jerked back into place. "Why?"

"Now that the D.A.'s people have been through it, we should take a look ourselves."

"I don't know..."

"I'll go by myself if you want, but I think it would be a good idea for you to come along."

He was right, of course. She couldn't stay away forever. But the thought of returning to the place where the whole nightmare had begun was almost more than she could contemplate. She consoled herself with the thought that Flynn would be with her.

They walked the short distance to the block where she lived. Her apartment house was about halfway down. Built in the years before World War II, it had a solidness to it that newer buildings lacked.

Although she had been away only a few days, Constance had the disconcerting sense of returning from a long journey. Small details that she had always taken for granted suddenly jumped out at her.

When the doorman smiled at them, she smiled back, grateful for the human touch.

"Good to see you, Miss Lehane," he said gently. Obviously he knew, but then it was likely everyone in the building did. First there had been the police and the ambulance, then her own absence and the stories in the media and then the police again to search. Heaven only knew what they were saying about her.

A small, plump woman got into the elevator, escorted by her Pomeranian. She stared intently at Constance, apparently storing up every possible item of interest for later use. When they stopped at her floor, she scampered off quickly and disappeared down the hall.

Constance stifled a sigh. She refused to give in to her anger at the injustice of it all, even though the temptation was great. When they reached her floor, she got out first and indicated the way to her apartment.

"It's the one on the end," she said.

Flynn nodded. The building was well maintained but generally impersonal. The woman with the Pomeranian notwithstanding, it was the kind of place that attracted busy people who weren't home much.

The chances of anyone having heard something that night and being willing to talk about it were slim, but he made a mental note to check it out.

The door to her apartment was securely locked, but lacked the usual red seal with black lettering that indicated a crime scene. Ben was keeping his part of the bargain. No crime was presumed to have occurred, at least not so far.

Constance unlocked the door and stepped aside to let Flynn go in first. Etiquette be damned—she wasn't walking into that place cold. He switched the hall lights on and beckoned to her.

"Come on, everything looks fine."

She followed him in gingerly and glanced around. A quick sweep was enough to make several subtle changes jump out at her: books slightly ajar on a shelf, for instance, couch pillows in a different order and so on. But there was nothing to indicate the police had conducted a thorough search.

"They must not have done much," she said.

Flynn stood with his suit jacket pushed back, his hands on his hips, surveying the living room. It was a pretty room, light and inviting without being gimmicky. The predominant colors were white and peach, something he would ordinarily never have thought of but which seemed to work here.

The couch was big and no-nonsense, it looked as though it had actually been made for sitting on. The lights were similarly functional, intended for reading by rather than merely illuminating the furniture. The side tables were old, made of pine and respectably battered. Along one wall was a pine armoire that was closed but that he bet held a TV and stereo—the wires coming out of the back were a clue. The opposite wall held shelves for books, hundreds of them, all sizes and varieties. He thought of all the apartments and houses he'd been in where there wasn't a book in sight and smiled. In his own apartment there was a constant danger of injury from the piles of books left over everything. They grew beside the bed, next to his desk, in the breakfast nook, everywhere. He couldn't imagine living without books and was glad to see Constance didn't try.

In front of the couch was the marble coffee table. It was a good piece, made of green-veined marble that shouldn't have suited the feminine room but somehow did. Perhaps because of the extreme hardness of the stone, little had been done to ornament it. The sculptor, for it looked more like a piece of sculpture than of furniture, had merely smoothed and polished it. As a result the corners were sharp.

On the floor of the living room was a dhurrie rug. A dark, oblong stain spread across it near the coffee table. Two glasses lay on the rug. The scene appeared exactly as Constance had described it, but Flynn wanted to make sure.

"Is anything different from the way it was when you last saw this room?" he asked.

She told him about the books and the couch pillows, then shook her head. "That's about it."

"So there weren't visible signs of the struggle aside from the upset glasses?"

"Not really. Everything happened very quickly and, as you can see, there's not a lot of furniture or other things around to be disturbed."

He didn't say that some of the books could have been knocked off the shelves or maybe the dried flower arrangement on a side table or even a lamp, but he thought it.

"Let's check out the rest of the place," he said.

For a Manhattan apartment it was large, but that was typical of the prewar buildings. In addition to the living room there was a bedroom, a bath and an eat-in kitchen. The bedroom was simply and attractively done in white and blue-gray with a four-poster bed, more bookshelves and an old mirrored vanity that looked Victorian. Nothing in the room appeared to have been touched, although one drawer of the vanity was slightly ajar.

Constance looked grim as she shut it. "I can't believe I'm saying this but I really wish the police had done a much more thorough search. Maybe that would have convinced them I have nothing to hide."

"Don't kid yourself," Flynn said as they walked back toward the kitchen. "They went through this place with a fine-tooth comb. Morgenstern insists on that, and he's no one to cross. He says you're squeaky-clean."

"Does that mean he's going to forget the whole thing?" she asked without much hope that would turn out to be the case. If there had been any chance of that, Flynn would already have told her.

"Nope," he said matter-of-factly. "It means we have one week, if we're lucky, to come up with an explanation for why Lewis Sheffield did what he did. If we can give Ben a plausible reason, he'll walk away no matter what the family says or does. But if we can't, he's got no choice but to go to the grand jury."

"Then I'll just tell the grand jury that I didn't do it," Constance said. The anger was rising in her again. It was all so damn unfair.

"No," Flynn said quietly, "you won't. As your attorney, I will advise you not to respond to questions at that time."

Constance turned and looked at him, her eyes incredulous. "Why on earth would you do that?"

He sighed. To him the point was elementary, but he kept forgetting that there were complete novices to the law who had no real idea of how it worked, only a blind faith that it would somehow protect them. That was a nice thought, but it happened to ignore reality.

"Because," he said patiently, "if you testify before the grand jury, the prosecution will have the right to cross-examine you. The odds are Morgenstern himself will handle this one, but even if he doesn't, he has plenty of sharp-toothed assistants to do the job for him. They'll be looking to draw you out in any and every possible way in order to get ammunition to use against us in a trial. We could be forced to reveal our defense in advance, thereby giving the prosecution time to construct a response to it. In purely strategic terms, you never show your hand prematurely."

"Doesn't that make a mockery of the whole grand jury system?" Constance demanded. "I mean isn't the idea that the grand jury hears evidence both for *and* against indictment before making up its mind?"

"Sure, it is," Flynn agreed. "But in actual fact, it usually doesn't work like that. The grand jury hears why the prosecution thinks it has a case and that's it. If the argument is strong enough, the jurors vote to indict. *Then* the defense goes to work."

"That's not right," Constance insisted. "People shouldn't be put through the hell of a trial just because grand jurors didn't have the whole story."

Flynn shrugged. "Maybe not, but realistically that's how the system works. Anyway, we can derail the whole thing by coming up with a plausible explanation for Sheffield's behavior. Ben smells a snow job and he's willing to dump the whole thing. But he's got to have a reason."

"We won't find it here," Constance said glumly. "I'd like to pick up a few things, but that shouldn't take long."

Flynn nodded. "Good. We got lucky on the way in, but there's no guarantee that media won't get wind that you're here. The sooner we're out, the better."

In fact, it wasn't soon enough.

As they came out of the building, Flynn carrying the suitcase Constance had packed, they saw a panel truck parked in front. A microwave dish antenna was on its roof and the call letters of a network flagship station were emblazoned on its side.

"*Oh, no,*" Constance murmured.

Flynn moved quickly, placing himself between her and the van. As he did so, a woman charged toward them. She was in her thirties, very slender with blond hair, a Miss America smile and eyes like a hungry wolfhound. There was a microphone gripped in the hand she shoved under Constance's nose.

"Miss Lehane, I'm Mary Jane Fairfax from Worldwide Broadcasting. Do you have any comment about the death of Lewis Sheffield?"

Flynn's hand was firm on Constance's arm as he kept them both moving. Without looking directly at the reporter he said, "We have no comment at this time."

Her attention momentarily diverted, Mary Jane said, "You're Flynn Corbett, aren't you? One of the most high-powered and best-known defense attorneys in New York. Are you convinced of Miss Lehane's innocence?"

Flynn stopped. He looked straight at the Minicam trailing after them on the shoulder of a hapless cameraman, and matched Mary Jane high-voltage smile for high-voltage smile. "Absolutely. Miss Lehane is completely without fault in the death of Lewis Sheffield. Any attempt to claim otherwise is a gross miscarriage of justice. Now, if you'll excuse us . . ."

"Do you expect a grand jury indictment?" she pressed, dodging in front of them. Flynn looked around her and hailed a passing cab. The driver hit the brakes and craned his neck out the window to see what was going on.

"No comment," Flynn said.

"What about you, Miss Lehane? You must know the Sheffield family is determined to make you pay."

Constance bit back the retort that sprang to her lips and stared straight ahead. The cab wasn't more than fifteen feet away. She could make it that far.

"Were you sleeping with him, Miss Lehane?'

"No comment," Flynn said.

"Was it a lovers' quarrel?"

"No comment."

"Did you find out he was dumping you for Delia Russell?"

Flynn pushed Constance into the cab and put her suitcase in the front seat, getting in beside her. Mary

Jane was right up against the door, one hand thrust out to keep it open.

"Unless you want to lose that," Flynn said quietly, "get out of the way."

She looked at him uncertainly for a moment before deciding he was serious. With a muttered expletive she stepped back. He slammed the door.

"Hit it," he said to the cabbie.

The driver needed no further encouragement. He put the pedal to the metal and dive-bombed into traffic, leaving shrieking horns and screaming humanity in his wake. Doing at least fifty miles per hour, he ignored the road and gave his passengers his undivided attention, turning to look over his shoulder at them.

"Way to go! I watch that broad on the tube all the time. She's a real pain in the butt."

A truck coming out of a side street drove halfway up on the sidewalk to avoid hitting them. The driver gestured murderously out the window as they sped by.

"Thanks," Flynn said calmly. "You can let us off at Park and Sixty-fifth."

The cabbie turned back to consider the road but not without a further glance at Constance. "Hey, you that lady who did in the rich dude?"

Constance relaxed her grip slightly on the edge of the seat and said, "I didn't do him in. It was an accident."

"Oh, yeah? Jeez, you can't be too careful these days. Accidents happen all the time. Just a couple of weeks ago my cousin Salvatore was coming out of a bar over on Third and whatta you think? Some crazy in a Ford with Jersey license plates goes tearing by, almost takes his legs off. Does the creep stop to see what happened? Nah. He just keeps going, heading for the tunnel.''

"That's too bad," Constance murmured.

"Yeah," the driver said in passing. "Anyway, the really weird part is that, at the same time this is happening, Sal's wife, Winnie, goes to open a bottle of ginger ale from the fridge and the whole damn top comes flying off, practically explodes in her face. I'm not kidding, it broke the light over the sink, it hit so hard. He coulda' been killed, she coulda' ended up blind, and all at the same time. Go figure."

"I trust Sal and Winnie are all right now," Flynn said.

"As good as, I guess. Say, you a lawyer?"

"I'm afraid so."

"Whatta you think, the thing with the ginger ale, could Winnie sue or something?"

"Not unless she suffered some kind of actual harm."

"What kind? I mean, she can still see and all but she was real shook-up. What about some kind of psychological impair—what they call it? After all, she'll probably never be able to drink ginger ale again, and she really liked that stuff."

"I wouldn't suggest it," Flynn said firmly. "Tell Winnie to drink orange juice. It's better for her, anyway."

"I thought you lawyer guys liked to sue."

"The courts are overcrowded, the system is cracking at the seams and the real criminals are getting away scot-free. That's not a good situation, don't you agree?"

"Yeah, I guess so. Still, I don't think Winnie's ever going to be the same. She's got woman problems."

"They're probably not related to a lack of ginger ale. Perhaps if Sal spends less time in Third Avenue bars and more time at home..."

They swerved inward toward the curb, terrifying a slender young man who had made the mistake of trying to cross the street with the light.

"That's what I told him," the cabbie said. "I said, Sal, you gotta stop the boozing. The next guy might not miss. You wanna be splattered all over the sidewalk or what? You know what he said?"

"Let me guess. He said in New York, who would notice anyway?"

"Hey, that's right. You're pretty smart for a guy in a suit." The cab rammed to a stop at, miraculously, their destination. "That'll be six fifty-five."

Flynn paid him, added a tip, and helped Constance out of the cab. She stood on the sidewalk and watched it disappear with a bemused look on her face.

"What was all that about?"

"All what?" Flynn replied as they started walking west. Dominique's hotel was only a few blocks away. Discretion dictated that they be let off somewhere other than right there.

"I know cabbies have a reputation for being talkative, but do you get into conversations like that very often?"

Flynn thought for a moment before he said, "Yes, as a matter of fact, I do. I'm not sure why but I always end up talking with whoever I happen to be with."

"I know why."

"Why?"

"You have a nice face. It's strong and trustworthy, also there's something... approachable about it."

He stopped and looked at her. "Did I hear a compliment?"

Her cheeks warmed. "Don't let it go to your head."

Flynn chuckled softly. "I wouldn't dare." They had reached the hotel. He followed her through the revolving doors into the lobby. "What are your plans for the rest of the day?"

"I thought I'd take a nap, read a little, that sort of thing."

"No, really."

She sighed. This business of his being able to tell every time she bent the truth even the tiniest bit was getting tiresome.

"Dominique gave me a list of names of people who knew Lewis. I thought I might get in touch with some of them."

"Not on your own," Flynn said quickly. When she remained silent, he said, "I'm serious. I want you to promise me you won't go off by yourself. Besides the fact that I don't think you'd get very far, there's a chance it could be dangerous."

"You mean I might get into some kind of trouble? Gee whiz, I sure hope not."

"I mean worse trouble than you've already got," he said, ignoring her sarcasm. "The Sheffields are nobody to mess with, not unless you really know what you're doing."

"And you do?"

"Yes," he said flatly, "I do. Listen, the block I grew up on in Hoboken, half the guys ended up doing time for something or other. They all had the same problem. They thought life owed them anything they wanted. The Sheffields work the same way. They use fancier language and wear fancier clothes, but that doesn't change what's really going on. The bottom line is they figure they're entitled, for one reason or another, to anything and everything. The difference between them and a bunch of street punks is that the Sheffields have generations of money and power behind them. You go up against them alone, you're going to get stomped on, that's guaranteed."

"All I'm suggesting is that I talk to a few people."

"Not by yourself. You're not walking into a problem like that while I'm around to prevent it."

She tilted her head back slightly, the better to look at him. He was very tall, standing there in the hotel lobby with the sunlight from the windows gleaming off his ebony hair. He seemed very serious, even worried. About her. The idea warmed her somehow.

"Sir Flynn," she said lightly in an effort to mask her own confusion. He was her lawyer, nothing more. She needed to work a little harder at remembering that.

"Yeah, if you want. Anything so long as you promise me."

"All right, all right, anything to make you stop." She took a deep breath. "I promise."

"Good. Look, is one of those people Dominique told you about the headmaster at Lewis's prep school, by any chance?"

Constance nodded. "She did mention him."

"Okay, as soon as I can get away, we'll take a drive up there and talk with him. Also, we'll check out the others but we'll do it together. In the meantime there's something only you can do. I need a list of people who could be character witnesses on your behalf. They should know you but not be related to you.''

At her look of alarm he went on quickly. ''It occurred to me that while Morgenstern's asking for proof that Lewis could have done what you say he did, we should also be giving him proof that you *couldn't* have done what the family says you did. They're trying to paint you as a liar, a gold digger and violent to boot. We've got to counteract that.''

''I'll do the best I can,'' Constance murmured. ''But with the family's reputation being what it is, won't people be afraid to testify on my behalf?''

Flynn had been hoping she wouldn't think of that. He nodded grimly. ''Probably, but we'll worry about that when we get to it. First the list.''

The elevator opened in front of them. He held the door as she got in but did not join her. ''I'll touch base with you later. Right now I've got to get back to the office.''

He watched her face, white and strained, until the two halves of the door met and shut it out. Only then did he turn and walk quickly from the lobby.

The autopsy report should be on his desk by now. The details of how an individual had died were hardly his favorite reading, but for once he was eager to get at it. He was going to *know* Lewis Sheffield if he had to start with his corpse and work back to the man he had been when he was alive. He was going to know what the guy thought and did and yearned for and dreamed of. And then he was going to use it all to stop the Sheffields once and for all.

He was that mad.

"Flynn," his parish priest had said to him on more than one occasion, "you've a keen mind and a strong will. They'll carry you far in life. But don't forget to listen to your heart. It's all right to feel, you know, even if the feelings aren't always comfortable."

Old Father Hanrahan probably wouldn't have listed deadly cold rage among the feelings Flynn should cultivate, but it would do. For a start.

Chapter 9

Constance put her pen down with a sigh. She leaned back in the chair and rubbed her eyes. The stress of trying to come up with the names of people who would testify on her behalf was taking a toll. Who could she ask to perform such a service? Who could she trust?

She had lived in New York for seven years and had met a large number of people, but of all of them there were only a few she could say actually knew her. Most were no more than casual acquaintances.

There were exceptions, of course. She glanced down at the list, studying the names. Phil Stevens was the first. Her boss was a solid, unshakable man with a top-notch reputation. If she wanted anyone speaking for her, it was him.

Also on the list were the names of several of her co-workers with whom she had shared tough assignments and the sort of social life that develops among people who have been in the trenches together.

Farther down the list were the names of the few men she had dated. That there were so few made her realize how small a part dating had played in her life. All the men had been perfectly pleasant; if she'd been looking for a casual relationship, even one that might grow serious later, she would have had no problem. But her sights were always higher. She wanted a man her heart would recognize not eventually but immediately. A man she could commit herself to, body and soul. A man like—

Oh, no, you don't, said the little voice in the back of her mind. *You're not falling into that one.* Flynn was her lawyer, plain and simple. She had to be nuts to start thinking of him in any other way.

So she was nuts. Under the circumstances, she probably should have expected it.

She got up from the small writing desk and switched on the TV, seeking diversion. A moment later she regretted it. Her own face leapt out at her, looking scared and defiant. Next to her was Flynn. She stared at him, surprised by the steely anger in his eyes.

Mary Jane Fairfax pushed forward, microphone in hand. "Was it a lovers' quarrel?" she demanded of Constance.

"No comment," Flynn said.

"Did you find out he was dumping you for Delia Russell?"

Cut to taxi pulling away from curb.

Cut to studio.

Mary Jane Fairfax, elegantly coiffed and made up, smiled into the camera. "The whereabouts of Miss

Lehane remains unknown. A spokesman for District Attorney Morgenstern's office said the investigation continues into the death of Lewis Sheffield.''

She turned to the blow-dried man seated next to her at the anchor's desk. ''Over to you, Jim.''

Jim grinned back and segued into a story about a fire in the Bronx that had killed four.

Constance switched off the TV. It was either that or put her foot through it. Her hands were shaking, and she felt sick to her stomach.

Earlier she had thought that when she finished the list she would go out for a brief walk before dark. The late-afternoon sun was warm and inviting, but now the idea of enjoying it was inconceivable. She couldn't possibly go out; somebody might recognize her. Even alone in her hotel room, she felt horribly exposed. Worse yet, she understood without needing to be told that this was only the beginning. It could get much, much worse before it was over.

Standing in the center of the room, her arms wrapped around herself, she struggled to fight back tears. All her life she'd hated crying. Her sister could cry beautifully, but Constance had never mastered that particular talent. When she cried, she did it messily. Her eyes turned red, her nose ran, and she felt like a damn fool. Also, she never had a handkerchief.

She went into the bathroom and found a box of tissues, then sat down on the rim of the tub. The tears came in hot, salty rivulets. She cried until in the midst of her anguish it suddenly occurred to her that she was no longer crying for herself. She was crying for Lewis, whose life had made him cruel and violent, and who was dead as a result. The ability to cry for the man who had started her torment proved oddly comforting. It made her feel as though some essential part of herself that she hadn't been too aware of lately was still there, still strong and resilient despite everything.

She raised her head and looked at herself in the mirror. No doubt about it, she was a mess. Still, she smiled. Lewis was dead, there was nothing she could do to change that. But she could put him to rest the only way that was possible, by seeing him for the sad, unfortunate man he had been.

She turned the cold-water tap on full blast and washed her face vigorously. When she was done, she combed her hair and went back into the bedroom and called room service. She wasn't going out, nothing had happened to change that. But she was going to have a good meal and stop feeling sorry for herself. And before she went to bed that night, she was going to recite ten times—a hundred if need be—that Flynn was only her lawyer.

If she said it often enough, she might have a chance of believing it.

At the same time Constance was picking up the phone to call room service, Flynn was contemplating the remains of a pepperoni wedge with the air of a man confronted by a distasteful object who can't quite remember how it came into his possession.

Oh, right, he'd asked Helen to get him something to eat when he got back to the office, then he'd gotten embroiled in the autopsy report and forgotten all about it.

His stomach, shameless thing that it was, growled. ˙ seemed to think the soggy, tomato-sauce-stained sandwich was actually edible, but Flynn himself knew better.

"Eat that, boyo," he muttered to himself, "and you'll be lining up for a visit to Doc Tanaka's."

Tanaka was the city's medical examiner. He was sixty-five years old and stood at five foot two. Weighing in at just over a drop of water, he smoked the kind of cigars no self-respecting bum would pick up off the sidewalk. He also boxed, bantamweight, at one of the city's few remaining genuine gyms into which an aerobics instructor only stepped upon pain of dismemberment.

Ordinarily defense attorneys made a habit of questioning the credentials, professionalism and manhood, or womanhood, of any medical examiner on the grounds that their testimony was usually key to getting a client indicted. But even Flynn had to admit that Tanaka was good. He'd certainly done a job on Lewis. Flynn resisted thoughts of putting Humpty Dumpty back together again and returned to his study of the autopsy report's summary.

Lewis had died from a lateral blow to the left occipital lobe of the brain, causing subcutaneous bleeding . . . depressing the skull in the region, resulting in a terminal infarction . . . The shape of the blow and the overall nature of the injuries indicated a blunt object. The deceased's stomach contents were consistent with the recent consumption of a meal as described by witnesses at the restaurant and by Miss Lehane. Alcohol content of the bloodstream was minimal. No indication of drugs were found. All body organs were intact and healthy. No pathology of any kind was present.

In short, Lewis Sheffield should have gone on living for years instead of winding up stone-cold dead under Dr. Tanaka's scrutiny.

Under the section entitled Conclusions the good doctor had written: "Death resulted from an injury to the brain caused by a blunt object. The angle of injury indicates that the deceased was turned slightly away from the object at the time the blow occurred. There are no scratches, bruises or other injuries to indicate the presence of a struggle prior to death."

Flynn let the autopsy report fall onto the desk. He cursed under his breath. Tanaka had only been doing his job, but he'd done a real number on Constance in the process. Sure, the report could be read as backup for her assertion that Lewis fell against the coffee table. The table certainly qualified as a heavy object, and the corners were blunt. In falling, Lewis could easily have had his head turned slightly away. The absence of any sign of a struggle was hardly surprising, given that Lewis was far stronger than Constance and certainly able to prevent her from harming him.

But a far different scenario was also possible, one in which no struggle occurred. One that had Constance wielding an object against an unsuspecting Sheffield. One that had her stone guilty of his murder.

Briefly Flynn considered the possibility that the Sheffield family had gotten to Tanaka, but he rejected the idea. The medical examiner was a lot of things—tough, demanding, arrogant. But he was so far from corrupt that it didn't even bear thinking about.

Which was too bad, because a thing like that would have been ready-made for Flynn to run with. Instead, he was back to square one, looking for an explanation for Lewis's seemingly uncharacteristic actions.

He was sitting there, thinking about what to do next, when the problem was solved for him. Helen stuck her head in the door. Her face was slightly flushed, and she looked almost excited, or as close to it as he'd ever seen.

"Charles Sheffield is on the phone," she said.

Flynn stared at her before abruptly straightening. He reached for the handset at the same moment that she discreetly withdrew.

"Mr. Sheffield," Flynn said coolly, "what can I do for you?"

"Any number of things, Mr. Corbett," Charles responded. His tone was equally cool, with a patrician undercurrent that made it clear he understood the significance of their disparate origins, pedigrees, outlooks and so on, even if that had somehow managed to elude Flynn himself. "However," he went on, "I doubt you're likely to approve of many of them. It's unfortunate that you should choose to represent someone like Constance Lehane."

"I don't see it that way, Mr. Sheffield. My client is an upstanding young woman who got caught up in a terrifying situation. What happened to your brother was unfortunate, but it was an accident."

"So Miss Lehane claims, but she also claims my brother attacked her, which is total nonsense. Lewis was an attractive man, well-known in the community. Hardly the type to lack for feminine companionship."

Flynn frowned slightly. Charles sounded as though he were reciting something, if not against his will then certainly with reluctance and possibly even resent-ment. Those weren't his words coming out of his mouth—of that, Flynn was sure.

"It's a common mistake," Flynn said, "to think a lack of sex can lead to rape. Rape is a crime of vio-lence, pure and simple. Are you saying your brother wasn't a violent man?"

"I'm saying nothing," Charles responded angrily. The thin veneer of courtesy he had managed to main-tain threatened to crack. He took a deep breath, struggling to contain himself.

"I have no interest," he continued, "in engaging in a debate with you. I am calling only because my mother has expressed a desire to meet with you."

Flynn's eyebrows shot up. Another few inches and they would have hit the ceiling.

"You understand there's a potential conflict of in-terest involved here, since I represent Constance Le-hane."

"I'm also an attorney, Mr. Corbett," Charles said. At least those were the words that came out. Flynn had no trouble translating them. *So don't try that phony conflict-of-interest crap on me because we both know it's a crockfull.*

"If Miss Lehane was already under indictment for my brother's murder, as she should be, we would not be meeting with you. However, as that has not yet oc-curred, my mother believes such a meeting should take place." Grudgingly Charles added, "She informs me that she has great respect for you as an attorney. Ap-parently she has followed your career with some in-terest through the newspapers and she regrets seeing you enmesh yourself in a case that can only do you harm.''

Flynn allowed himself one of his famous shark smiles, the kind prosecuting attorneys dreaded. ''Thank your mother for her concern,'' he said smoothly, ''and tell her I'd be happy to meet with her.''

''She'll expect you at her apartment at 8:00 p.m.'' Charles said through gritted teeth. Being his mother's errand boy was bad enough; being Flynn's was intolerable. ''Be there.'' He hung up.

Flynn laughed as he put the phone down. He bounded out of the chair and paced over to the windows, where he stood looking down at the street. Helen found him that way.

''Everything all right?'' she asked.

''I think we just got a break or are about to. I'm meeting with Elizabeth Sheffield this evening.''

Helen looked puzzled. ''Why would you want to do that?''

''Because it isn't too often the enemy invites you into their camp. They're the key to what made Lewis tick, I'm sure of it. If I'm going to get a handle on him, I've got to understand his family first.''

''If you say so,'' Helen murmured, still skeptical, ''but I hope you'll be careful.''

''Yes, Mother.''

''All right, I won't worry. What should I tell Miss Lehane if she calls?''

''Tell her I'm betraying her trust and going over to the other side—what do you think you should tell her?''

Helen smiled. "Mighty touchy these days, aren't we?"

"Maybe you are but—"

"There, there, it'll all be fine. She's a lovely young woman, and it's about time you got serious."

Flynn's color faded. He stared at his secretary, who gazed back at him blandly. "What're you talking about? Constance Lehane is a client."

"Of course she is. Wear your coat. It's getting cold outside."

Flynn thought he'd get the last word; he almost always did. But before he could figure it out, Helen was gone. He was left to wonder if he was that transparent to anyone else. Constance, for instance.

Chapter 10

Elizabeth Sheffield's apartment was on Fifth Avenue overlooking Central Park. The evening being pleasant, Flynn walked up. Arriving as he did on foot, he was subjected to the particularly intense scrutiny of the doorman. In most buildings the doormen were either elderly gentlemen augmenting their pensions or young men who hadn't yet found a better niche for themselves. This guy didn't fall into either category. He stood several inches over six feet tall, putting him on eye level with Flynn. His hair was close-cropped, his eyes sharp, and his physique that of a linebacker who'd kept himself in top-notch shape. Everything about him shrieked professional. He stood up from behind his desk as Flynn approached.

"May I help you, sir?" The words were polite; the tone was not. It said that if Flynn was up to any funny stuff, and odds were that he was, he was going to remember this as the worst night of his life.

"My name is Flynn Corbett. I'm here to see Mrs. Sheffield. She's expecting me."

"Identification?"

Flynn frowned. This was beyond the usual routine in even the strictest of buildings. Not that the years at Harvard didn't count, but when push came to shove he was still strictly Hoboken.

"What's it to you?" he demanded.

"Standard procedure. No ID, no admittance."

Flynn frowned but kept a grip on himself. He might not like it, but it really wasn't that big a deal. He fished in his pants pocket for his wallet and flashed his driver's license.

The incredible hulk stared at it for several moments before nodding. "Okay." He reached behind into the desk and withdrew a handheld metal detector, the kind airport security guards used to go over anyone who flunked the standard walk-through.

"Hold your arms away from your sides."

Flynn stood, arms down and stared at him. "You gotta be kidding."

"Standard procedure."

"Like hell." He had his usual .32 snub-nose in the shoulder holster under his jacket, but that wasn't the point. The gun was one hundred percent legal—nobody could argue with that. The point was that he was starting to really dislike this guy's face.

"Forget it," Flynn said. "Last I heard, Elizabeth Sheffield wasn't the Queen of England. She wants to see me, she can come down to my office."

He turned and walked out the door.

The big guy followed. "Wait a sec'. You said she's expecting you."

"Yeah."

"She's not going to like it if you don't show."

"I'm really broken up about that."

He raised his hand to hail a cab. Nice night or not, he'd had enough exercise. He'd head back to the office and get in a few more hours' work.

The doorman furled his brow, proving he was capable of some emotion other than suspicion. "Look, I was just following orders."

Flynn lowered his hand. He turned and looked at the other man. "Whose?"

"Charles Sheffield's," the man admitted. "He said you were coming by and to let you in but not to make it too easy. He kinda wanted you to get the runaround."

A glimmer of genuine interest appeared in the small eyes. "He doesn't like you, you know."

"I'm crushed," Flynn said. "I'm also carrying." He opened his jacket slightly and flashed the gun. Okay, the gesture was a *little* immature but what the hell. "You wanna make something of it?"

"Not me," the man said hastily. He backpedaled several steps toward the door. "I did what I was supposed to, pretty much. Mr. Sheffield never said anything about you being armed or what I should do about it if you were."

"Chuckie has no imagination," Flynn said as he walked toward the door. The man held it open for him nicely. Flynn thanked him just as politely and waited while he got on the house phone.

"Go on up," he said when he replaced the receiver. "Mrs. Sheffield is on the top floor."

The whole top floor, as it turned out. She had one of those apartments where the elevator opened straight into the entry hall. It featured a couple of good Impressionist paintings, a Louis XV side table, an Oriental rug so thick and plush that it rippled underfoot and a vase Flynn guessed was Ming dynasty. And that was just for starters.

Along one side of the hall were double bronze doors incised with Byzantine crosses. They could have been the entrance to a throne room and in a sense they were. The major domo in this case was a Chinese woman of indeterminate age, except that she was very old, dressed in the traditional black trousers and white high-necked shirt of an *amah,* or child's nurse. Her sparse white hair was gathered up in a bun. Her moon-shaped face was motionless except for the eyes that swept Flynn with an all-encompassing scrutiny.

She did not speak but merely stepped aside for him to enter. Beyond was a large, stately room with marble walls and an ornate ceiling supported by Corinthian columns. At the far end of the room, near a brace of floor-to-ceiling windows that overlooked the park, sat Elizabeth Sheffield.

What Flynn knew of her personal history told him that she had to be in her seventies if she was a day, but there was little in her appearance to confirm that. She was a small, slender woman with golden hair, blue eyes, and porcelain skin, dressed in a simple shift made of raw silk. Except for large diamond earrings and an equally sized diamond ring, she wore no jewlry.

Studying her, Flynn presumed the almost unlined quality of her skin was the result of face-lifts. But when she offered him her hand and he glanced down at it, he began to wonder. Hands, like necks, still defied the magic of the plastic surgeon. They were generally dead giveaways of age. Yet Elizabeth Sheffield's hand, while not so youthful as her face, was smooth and unspotted. Her nails were buffed, not painted. Like everything else about her, her hand smelled faintly of Chanel.

"Mrs. Sheffield," he said, inclining his head slightly.

She gestured to the chair beside the couch where she sat. "Mr. Corbett, so nice of you to come by." Her voice was soft and slightly breathless with a faint tinge of her Southern girlhood in it.

Flynn settled into the chair and looked at her directly. "When your son issued his kind invitation, I couldn't resist. Curiosity overcame me."

Elizabeth Sheffield laughed. Like so much else about her, the laugh belonged to a far younger woman. "Frankness is always so refreshing," she said, "probably because it is also so rare. I think I'm going to like you, Mr. Corbett."

Flynn sighed. He shook his head regretfully. "I doubt it, ma'am. You're going to try to convince me not to represent Constance Lehane, but I can tell you going in that you won't succeed. I'm sorry about what happened to Lewis but I'm convinced Miss Lehane is not to blame."

Elizabeth heard him out calmly. When he had finished, she gestured to the *amah* who had been hovering a discreet distance away. "Tea, Li-ping," sh* directed. Looking at Flynn, she added, "Or perhaps Mr. Corbett would prefer something stronger?"

"Tea is fine," he assured her.

Elizabeth nodded to the Chinese woman, who promptly withdrew. When they were alone again, she said, "Li-ping is invaluable to me. I first met her in Hong Kong more than fifty years ago. We've been together ever since."

"What took you to Hong Kong?" Flynn asked. A little small talk couldn't hurt. Besides, he was, as always, plagued by his genuine interest in anyone and everyone. Fifty years ago Elizabeth Sheffield would have been about twenty, and World War II would have been on the near horizon. What had drawn her from the safety of home to what was shortly to be the front line of battle?

"I was touring the Far East with a song-and-dance troupe," she said matter-of-factly. "Arnie's American Angels, it was called. Arnie was the producer. We played all the top spots—Bombay, Rangoon, Bangkok. Hong Kong was our last stop."

"And that's where you met Li-ping?"

"That's right. She was ten years old. Her parents had sold her into a brothel but she'd run away and was in the streets, dreadfully dirty and hungry. I took her in, and she's stayed with me ever since."

"That was kind of you," Flynn murmured.

"No," Elizabeth Sheffield said firmly, "it wasn't. I am never kind. Li-ping appealed to me because she was worse off than I was. In her eyes I was important, powerful, even wealthy. She was marvelous for y ego. Besides, I was reasonably sure she would be al, and that has turned out to be the case."

"Are you always so direct?"

She nodded. "It's a luxury I feel I have earned."

Flynn looked at her thoughtfully. "You're not what I expected," he said.

She laughed softly. "I won't ask you to elaborate. I know exactly what people think of me, and it is far from flattering. Probably the kindest thing I've been called is a gold digger, and that was back in my youth. It's gotten a whole lot worse since then."

"You don't seem bothered by it," Flynn observed. On the contrary, she seemed positively serene. The woman radiated not only self-confidence but self-contentment, as well. Elizabeth Sheffield was well satisfied with her life. Moreover, she took full credit for it.

Nothing wrong with that, Flynn supposed, except that it seemed strange coming from a woman whose youngest son was so recently dead. She was either close to superhumanly good at concealing grief or Lewis's demise just hadn't hit her that hard.

Or had it? Behind the smile and the almost girlish manner the blue eyes were hard. Elizabeth Sheffield wasn't used to being thwarted. The novelty of her current experience didn't make it any more appealing.

Li-ping returned with the tea. It was oolong, dark and bitter, served in Meissen cups so finely made as to be almost transparent. Flynn sipped his appreciatively. He liked things that were well-done whatever the circumstances.

"I hope you won't mind," Elizabeth said, eyeing him over the rim of her cup, "but I asked a few people to stop in this evening to meet you."

"Who are they?" Flynn asked. He wasn't surprised. Having gone so far as to invite him into her home, she obviously intended to do whatever was necessary to change his mind about Constance. He was merely curious as to who she intended calling upon.

"Friends of Lewis's," she said. "People who really knew him." She put her cup down and leaned forward slightly. Her eyes locked on Flynn's. "Lewis was a fine, fine man. His death is a terrible tragedy, which we as his family will have to live with forever. I accept that, but what I cannot accept is his reputation being sullied in the way your Miss Lehane insists on doing. My son is dead, he cannot defend himself. I have no choice but to do so myself."

It was impressive, Flynn had to grant her that. If she was on the witness stand, where she might eventually be, a jury would be hard-pressed not to believe her. Exit Elizabeth Sheffield, queenly matriarch. Enter suffering mother channeling her grief into the defense of her son's honor. No doubt about it—it played well.

He sat back, crossed one leg over the other, and waited to see what would happen next.

Constance had just finished her dinner and wheeled the tray outside to be collected by room service. She was lying on the bed, reading one of the books she'd taken from her apartment, when there was a knock at the door.

Opening it, she found a worried Dominique. "May ome in for a moment?" the older woman asked.

"Of course," Constance said. "Is something wrong?"

"I'm afraid so." Dominique's hands were clasped together as she stepped into the room. Her black eyebrows, arched like the wings of a bird, were drawn tightly together. "The switchboard operator has reported several calls from people asking to be put through to you, and a few moments ago a television van pulled up in front. So far, no one from it has come inside, but they appear to be watching us."

Constance's face turned white. She had known there existed a possibility of her being found but she hadn't expected it to happen quite so soon. The hotel had been such a simple and immediate refuge that she hadn't thought much beyond it. Now she had no choice but to do so.

"I'll have to leave," she said quickly. "If they think I'm here, they'll keep trying to find me no matter how much disruption that causes."

"My staff is completely trustworthy," Dominique said. "They won't reveal that you're here."

"I know, but that won't matter. Your guests will be disturbed and inconvenienced. That isn't right."

Dominique couldn't argue with that but she still wasn't ready to give in. "There's no reason why you can't stay. I shall simply insist that you aren't here and if they don't leave, I shall call the police."

"They'll just camp out on the sidewalk. If I try to go in or out, they'll spot me." The thought of what would happen then was enough to make her stomach churn. Rather than give in to it she forced herself to smile reassuringly.

"Don't worry, I'll think of something. I'm just glad I found out so quickly."

"I wish there was something I could do," Dominique said. "This just isn't fair."

"It'll be over soon," Constance said, as much for her own sake as for Dominique's. She simply had to believe that.

Perhaps Dominique also believed it but she looked doubtful. She touched Constance's arm gently and said, "I think you had better call Flynn."

Constance nodded. Much as she would have liked to solve the problem on her own, she was stymied. She couldn't stay at the hotel or go to another, and her apartment was out of the question. What was left?

Reluctantly she reached for the phone.

Flynn unlocked his apartment door and stepped inside, switching off the alarm system. Without bothering to turn on any lights he walked across the entry hall into the living room. The curtains were open, affording a spectacular view of the New York skyline. He stood for a long moment, staring out at it.

It was close to midnight and he was undeniably tired, but there was no point in going to bed. He knew himself well enough to be sure that he wouldn't be able to sleep. The details of his meeting with Elizabeth Sheffield would keep him awake far into the night.

The woman came out with guns blazing, that was for sure. The friends she'd invited to "drop by" had been strictly heavy hitters. If somebody wanted to compile a list of the city's young elite, every one of the men he'd met that night would have to be on it. There were half a dozen in all, ranging in age from the up-

per twenties to the midthirties. All said they had
known Lewis personally, several had gone to school
with him and others had encountered him socially. The
general consensus was unanimous—Lewis was a great
guy, one of nature's noblemen, creative, hardwork-
ing and a top-notch bridge player to boot. One of the
men had even gone so far as to say he thought of Lewis
like a brother.

The little get-together had turned into an informal
wake for the deceased. Each of the men had gotten up
to give little speeches about what a great guy Lewis
had been while everyone nodded knowingly. Everyone, that is, except Flynn. He sat through the whole
experience virtually ignored after the initial introduc-
tions. No one tried to collar him directly, but all their
comments were, one way or another, meant for him.

Through it all Elizabeth Sheffield sat enthroned,
nodding her golden head from time to time and even,
on a few occasions, raising a lace-edged handkerchief
to blot away an invisible tear. By the time Flynn left,
he knew he had witnessed a demonstration of what
power really meant. All of the men had been uncomfortable, all would clearly have preferred to have been
somewhere else, but each had performed as promised. Elizabeth Sheffield had every reason to be satisfied.

Every reason except one—it hadn't worked. After
such an extraordinary display he was more convinced
than ever that something was rotten in the state of
Sheffield.

The red light was flashing on his answering ma
chine. He went over to it and pushed down the Pla
button. Constance's voice filled the room.

"I'm sorry to bother you but I've got a problem. Some reporters have found out that I'm staying at Dominique's. They're outside with a van now, and there may be more on the way. I don't really know what to do, so please give me a call."

Flynn cursed under his breath. He had no idea when she'd left the message but he had an uneasy feeling it hadn't been within the past few minutes. Hastily he punched in Dominique's number and asked for her directly, knowing he'd never get past the desk if he asked for Constance herself.

His call had been anticipated and he was put through almost at once to Dominique, who confirmed that it was indeed he.

"I'm so glad you've called," she said. "The news people did come into the lobby several hours ago, but we managed to convince them they had to leave. They're still outside, though."

"How's Constance holding up?" Flynn asked.

"She's a very strong young woman but she's frightened. Who wouldn't be?"

Flynn nodded grimly. He spoke a little longer with Dominique before the call was transferred to Constance's room. She answered on the first ring.

"Flynn, thank heavens."

He closed his eyes for a moment, drinking in the heartfelt relief in her voice. She couldn't have sounded like that unless she trusted him completely. He was grateful for that even as it made him a tad humble. Given the complexity of his feelings for her, trust had to be handled carefully.

"How are you?" he asked gently.

"All right, I guess, but I have to get out of here. This is terribly unfair to Dominique. The problem is I don't know where to go."

Flynn thought quickly. He could bring her back to his apartment, but his involvement in the case was well-known and reporters would naturally look there. Of his many friends and acquaintances in New York, there were at least several he could have imposed upon, but he was reluctant to do so. Like it or not he had to admit that he wanted Constance all to himself. Ben Morgenstern wouldn't be too happy, that was for sure, but too bad. Flynn wasn't feeling too charitably toward the D.A. these days.

"I'll be there in fifteen minutes," he said. "I'll come up through the underground garage. You go ahead and get packed, okay?"

"Okay," she said softly.

It was only after she hung up that it occurred to him she hadn't asked where they would be going. He could only hope that when she found out, she wouldn't get the wrong idea. Or the right one. Or—

The hell with it. He was a man first and a lawyer second. Maybe it was time to admit that.

Chapter 11

Constance was waiting for him when he arrived at her room. She was wearing gray trousers with a white turtleneck pullover and had a suede jacket over her arm. Behind her was the single suitcase she'd brought from her apartment.

She smiled when she saw him, but her eyes were shadowed and she said nothing. He took the suitcase and waited while she made sure the door had locked behind her.

"I left the key in the room," she said. "Dominique knows it's there. She'll wait until morning before she tells the reporters I've left."

A bellboy was holding the elevator for them to make sure there would be no other passengers. Flynn thanked him and pressed the button for the basement garage. He'd parked against the far wall, out of sight of anyone else who might be entering. Constance followed him until she caught sight of his car, then her step faltered. The distinctive chunky shape with its long, snub-nosed hood and high roof was unmistakable.

"A Checker?" she asked.

Flynn patted the hood affectionately. "Couldn't be anything else, could it? Built like a tank and runs like a dream. I got one of the last ones off the assembly line."

Constance couldn't help it; she laughed.

"What's so funny?" he demanded, looking wounded.

"You are. You should be driving a Jaguar or a Porsche, something that shrieks 'look how successful I am.' Instead, you're driving a car that says 'I don't give a damn.'"

"I *like* this car," he said as he put her suitcase in the spacious trunk. "It reminds me of the taxis in London, which happen to be one of the great accomplishments of Western civilization."

"That's true," Constance agreed. She waited as he unlocked the door, then slid into the front passenger seat. Flynn got in next to her. "Scrunch down a little," he said as he turned the key in the ignition.

She did as he said, discovering that the car's generous proportions provided more than just comfort; they completely concealed her. Flynn had brought a rakish, broad-brimmed hat with him. He pulled it down over his face as the car left the garage.

"Okay," he said a short time later when they were several blocks away from the hotel.

Constance sat back up. "Were they still there?"

Flynn nodded. "One van, no sign of anyone in it, but you can bet somebody's keeping an eye out. They'll probably wait until morning to attack."

"Good thing the cavalry got here so fast," she said. More seriously she added, "It did occur to me that it might be best to just talk to the reporters and be done with it."

"You wouldn't have been," Flynn said, "done with it, that is. They would have kept after you no matter what you did. If this does go to indictment, you'll talk. But right now the goal is to settle this as quickly and cleanly as possible. That means you don't want your face up on the TV screen for people to see and remember any more than can possibly be avoided."

"That's fine with me," Constance murmured. Now that the rush to get out of the hotel was over, fatigue was starting to sink in. She was having trouble keeping her eyes open. The car plowed along smoothly through the almost nonexistent traffic. The seat was wide and welcoming. All she had to do was put her head back a little and she'd slip right off into—

"Go to sleep," Flynn said softly. "I'll wake you when we get there."

Constance didn't answer, unless the soft flutter of her breath counted as a response.

Flynn shifted more comfortably in the seat and gunned the motor. Fifteen minutes later they were heading into the Bronx and beyond there, north out of the city.

Flynn had always liked Connecticut. He'd gone to camp there one summer at a place for "disadvantaged" kids, which had been like going to the other side of the moon. He smiled as he remembered how scared he'd been the first few nights, lying awake in his bunk listening to all the weird noises outside. Blaring horns, sirens and screams he could take, but not the rustlings and murmurings of Nature.

Nature, with a capital *N*, loomed up and hit him in the face that summer. All of a sudden he realized there was a world that wasn't made of concrete and asphalt, a world where people were just visitors and where every moment brought new surprises. He remembered lying facedown one day with his nose pressed against velvety soft moss, breathing in the scents of the earth and thinking that nothing could ever get any better.

Nothing ever had—as good as a few times, but never better. Ever since that time, he'd been pulled in two directions. The Big City was where the action was, but the countryside called to him just as potently. The solution was the cabin.

It was located three hours out of New York in the Litchfield County part of Connecticut. Twenty minutes off the closest major road and down a dirt lane, the house backed up to a pristine lake stocked with trout and bass. On the other side of rolling hills was the nearest town, a picture-postcard New England village complete with Colonial-era houses and a white-steepled church.

Not much of that was visible as Flynn drove through. Constance still slept peacefully in the seat beside him. She had barely moved since they'd left the city, which gave him a good idea of how tired she was. He slowed down as the car started up the winding unpaved road. The outside floodlights of the house came on automatically at dark, helping him find his way. He parked directly in front.

As he turned the engine off and opened the door, Constance stirred. She opened her eyes slowly and glanced around. "Where are we?"

"At the hideout," he said as he opened the door on her side. He smiled reassuringly. "I would have explained before we left the city, but you fell asleep."

She nodded and accepted his hand as he helped her out. The cold night air hit her suddenly, blasting her to full wakefulness. The wind carried a heavy hint of dampness. Thick clouds moved slowly in front of the moon. "I didn't think I was that tired." She looked around again, all her senses alert to the darkness, the different scents in the air and the absence of any human sounds that weren't their own.

"Where are we?" she asked again.

"Litchfield County. I keep this place for weekends. Lewis's old prep school is about half an hour from here. It occurred to me that since we wanted to visit the school anyway and you needed to get out of the city in a hurry, it made sense to come here."

He waited, half expecting her to disagree. When she didn't, he relaxed slightly. "Let me go ahead and unlock the door. Even with the lights, the path's a little rough."

She nodded but didn't comment any further as she followed him. He unlocked the door and flipped the lights on. Ahead was a "great room" that took up most of the first floor of the cabin. It was lined with hand-hewn birch logs and dominated by a fieldstone fireplace that rose to the ceiling. The furniture was big, overstuffed and comfortable. A braided rug lay on the floor, and several excellent American primitives hung on the walls. The air smelled of old wood smoke and pine.

"This is wonderful," Constance said softly. She looked at him. "Also unexpected. Did you buy this place or have it built?"

"I bought the land," Flynn explained. "Most of the construction I did myself. It took me five years, but I got it the way I wanted it."

"How did you know what to do? Did you teach yourself?"

"Some of it, but I used to work construction summers when I was in school. When it came to doing this, I was surprised how much I already knew."

She reached out gently and ran her hand over one of the walls, feeling the rough texture of the wood beneath her fingers. This man, this sophisticated, urbane, powerful man, had worked for five years to create a place of warmth and beauty hidden away from most of the world. He had done it with his own strength and sweat and with great patience, laying each log on top of another, planing the wood, hewing and polishing until at last it was done.

"Were you sorry when you finished?" she asked.

The question startled him. No one had ever asked it before. The few people who knew about the cabin presumed he was relieved to have it done. In fact, they were wrong. He had loved the labor involved in the building of it and wouldn't give that up easily.

"It isn't finished," he said. "It probably never will be. I've got plans for an addition eventually."

She smiled as though that made perfect sense to her. They stood for a long moment looking at each other.

Wisps of auburn hair drifted across her sleep-flushed face. Her eyes were wide and luminous. The soft full- ness of her mouth drew his gaze irresistibly. Flynn felt his body tighten. Desire rose hard and strong within him. Had he been eighteen, he would have acted on it. But he was a man not a boy, and the woman before him had been through a terrifying experience. She needed protection and reassurance, and he was damn well going to give it to her no matter what it cost.

Sir Flynn. He laughed at the memory.

"What's so funny?" Constance asked.

"Me, us, life in general." Ignoring her quizzical look, he said, "I forgot your bag in the car. Why don't you make yourself comfortable while I get it? The guest room is upstairs."

She nodded but made no move toward the stairs. Instead, she stood watching him as he let himself out the door. When he was gone, Constance let out a small sigh of relief. She had a few moments unobserved to gather her chaotic thoughts. What on earth was she going to do? Flynn had obviously acted from the sim- plest and most straightforward of motives when he brought her here. It was the logical place for her to be, given her need to escape the media and the cabin's nearness to Lewis's former school. The last thing he'd have in mind would be anything romantic. And if she let herself forget that, she'd only end up embarrass- ing both of them.

"Get a grip on reality, kid," she murmured. She heard Flynn coming up the walk and forced herself to move away from the door. He found her in the kitchen getting a drink of water from the tap.

"I hope you don't mind," she said. "I was thirsty."
Also curious to see more of the home he'd built. The
kitchen was big and cheerful, with its own stone fireplace that included a Colonial-style beehive oven. A
rough-hewn oak table and chairs were set nearby.
There were spacious counters and cabinets of the same
wood, and even a bookshelf loaded with cookbooks.

"You use these?" Constance asked.

"I like to cook," Flynn said a little defensively.
He'd been kidded about his cooking by the same people who wolfed it down every chance they got.

"So do I," Constance said. "Not that I get much
chance. The last few years everything's been so
rushed."

He knew what she meant. He'd be thirty-six on his
next birthday and he could honestly say he didn't
know where the time had gone. Sure, he'd accom-
plished a great deal, but there was a whole lot more
that was still hanging fire. Some kind of permanent
arrangement in his personal life, for instance. Maybe
even kids before too much longer.

Kids? Where on earth had that come from? "We
better get some rest," he said hastily.

Constance wondered what had made him look so
withdrawn all of a sudden but she knew better than to
ask. Despite her sleep in the car she was barely staying awake. Flynn carried the suitcase upstairs for her.
In the narrow hallway at the top of the stairs they
bumped into each other. Both moved away quickly.

"Sorry," Flynn said, not looking at her. It was
enough that he could smell the light floral scent of her
perfume and feel the warmth of her skin so close to his

own. "The bed's already made up," he went on. "Help yourself to anything you need."

Constance barely had time to murmur her thanks before he disappeared downstairs. A moment later she heard a door close toward the back of the cabin. She picked up her suitcase and went into the guest room. It was small, tucked away under the eaves, and furnished with a four-poster double bed covered by a bright quilt. There was a dresser and a washstand, as well a bookcase. A bath was off to one side.

She left her suitcase on the floor, taking out only what she needed to sleep in. The room was cool but it had been shut up for a time and smelled a little stuffy. She opened one of the two windows a crack and stood looking out into the darkness. Moonlight flashed on water. The scent of the nearby pine forest wafted in.

She climbed into the bed and pulled the covers up over herself. With the light off she could see the moon better. It drifted beyond the window, crossed by puffy clouds. She followed it for a time until her eyes grew too heavy to keep open any longer. The moon drifted, the spring wind blew over the lake, and Constance slept dreamlessly beneath the bright quilt.

Flynn also slept, downstairs in the master bedroom. He hadn't expected to, but barely had his head touched the pillow than he was out.

He awoke suddenly. It was still pitch-dark outside, but there was something...the wind in the trees, maybe, or the veiled, grayish light. He sat up and glanced at the clock beside the bed. It read 4:00 a.m.

Flynn muttered under his breath. He tossed the covers aside and stood up quickly. Lean and bronzed, naked except for the pair of pajama bottoms he'd pulled on the night before, he padded over to the windows. They were uncurtained and faced out toward the lake at the back of the house. Normally with a full moon he'd be able to see the lake, the pine copse behind it and so on. But at the moment he couldn't see much of anything except the stone patio directly beyond the house, and even that was heavily shadowed.

A glance at the sky showed why. The clouds that had begun gathering earlier in the night were a solid, gray mass now, backlit by a yellowish glare. As he watched, the first finger of lightning crackled across the sky. His eyes closed instinctively, but the image was so bright it seemed to sear the inside of the lids. Almost immediately the heavy rumble of thunder shook the house.

Flynn's hands clenched. He hated storms, but worse, he hated the fear they made him feel. He was a man, for God's sake. He'd never run away from a fight in his life, but let a little lightning and thunder start up and he could feel his guts turning to mush. His mother claimed it had something to do with an incident when he was seven years old. A terrible storm had blown over Hoboken, a bolt of lightning knocked the steeple off the church while the wind uprooted several trees and overturned a couple of cars. He'd slipped out on his own and then gotten stuck until the storm was almost over. All in all, he'd been lucky, suffering nothing more than some cuts and bruises from flying debris. He didn't even remember it, not consciously anyway. It probably had nothing to do with how he felt about this kind of weather. After all, he wasn't a kid anymore. He knew the lighting and thunder couldn't hurt him; he just didn't like them.

There was no sense trying to sleep until it was over. He opened the bedroom door and stepped out into the hall, where he listened for a moment. No sound from upstairs; Constance must be sleeping soundly. All the better—she needed the rest and he didn't need anyone hanging around to see how yellow he could be. Especially not her.

Which was not a line of thought he was going to follow up on. No sir, not him. Scared he might be, but he wasn't dumb. He was going to fix himself a nice little Scotch and water, the kind he hardly ever indulged in, find a good book, and put his feet up until the storm blew itself out. The hell with everything else.

The plan almost worked. He got the drink, found the book and even stretched out on the living-room couch where he debated whether or not to light the fire already laid in the fireplace in front of him. Why not? He got up, tossed a match on it and resumed his place. Score one for the city boy; the pile of tinder and logs ignited immediately.

He was sitting there trying to decide whether or not Elmore Leonard really was the best mystery writer ever, when he heard a faint sound behind him. Before he turned he knew what it was. Knew all the way down to the center and knew, too, that he'd been half waiting for this, hoping it would happen, maybe even daring it too.

Constance was standing at the bottom of the steps looking at him. She had on a plain white cotton nightgown that reached all the way to her ankles. Her hair was loose and fell over her shoulders. Her eyes were still heavy with sleep, and she seemed a little puzzled.

"Flynn . . . is something wrong?"

Her voice reached right through him. It was soft and slightly husky. Also, and this was undoubtedly inadvertent, it was very intimate.

He got up off the couch before he remembered all he was wearing were pajama bottoms. So why not; she was a grown woman, wasn't she? Okay, she'd been through a bad experience recently, but she had to know that she was safe with him, didn't she?

Was she?

"Everything's fine," he said hastily. "You should go back to bed."

"It's raining outside."

"Yeah, I know, there's a storm but it'll blow over soon. Go back to bed."

She raised a hand sleepily and pushed aside the wave of hair that was spilling over her face. "Why are you up?"

"Insomnia. Happens all the time." Liar—he usually slept like a log.

"Hmm, I think I'll fix some warm milk. Do you want any?"

He glanced down at the half-drunk Scotch and water on the table. The thought of pouring warm milk on top of that made him flinch. "No, thanks, I'm fine." Another lie. He was really chalking them up tonight.

"Okay." She wandered off toward the kitchen, where a moment later he heard pans rustling.

Just stay put, he thought. She'll fix the milk, drink it and go back upstairs. It's not a big deal. Sure, she's gorgeous, but so are a lot of other women you've known. Maybe not *as* gorgeous and not as smart and without that special mix of vulnerability and courage but still none of them were anything to sneeze at, either. Certainly none of them ever gave you any trouble, so what's the big deal now?

Another bolt of lightning ripped through the sky, sounding as though it was directly overhead. Flynn jumped. His hands tightened into fists, and he made a harsh sound deep in his throat.

In the kitchen Constance heard it. She wasn't sure where the sound came from but she didn't like it. It startled her enough that she splashed some of the milk on her hand.

It wasn't warm, it was hot. Hot enough to scald. She cried out and backed away toward the sink. The sudden shock of pain caught her off guard. For a moment she didn't know what to do.

Not that it mattered. She was picked right up off the floor, feet dangling, and carried directly over to the sink, where her hand was immediately plunged under cold water. Slammed up hard against Flynn's body, feet still groundless, she sucked in air and felt the pain ebb.

"Better?" he demanded.

She turned her head, meeting his eyes. Uh-oh, bad move. About the same as diving straight off a cliff.

"Flynn," she murmured, hardly breathing.

"Yeah?"

"My arm, it's fine now. You can..." Can what? She'd started out to say he could put her down, but the words had gotten lost in the general confusion that was roaring through her body. A flock of butterflies was doing the roller coaster boogie-woogie somewhere in her midsection. She felt alternately hot and cold, then strictly hot, very, very hot in a way that owed absolutely nothing to scalded milk. Her head fell back, the weight of her hair pulling it down. In a daze, she looked up at Flynn, taking in the smallest of details. His gaze was hooded, his mouth firm; there was a little nick on his chin where he'd cut himself shaving.

"Flynn . . ." He heard her say his name again, but it was different this time, soft with desire.

Slowly he lowered her to the floor. Sliding along the hard length of him, she felt his arousal and gasped, not with surprise but in simple relief that they were both, in their different ways, in the same state.

She needed him so badly. It was as though a stranger had taken control of her body. Someone without all the usual cautions and restraints that normally governed her. Someone without fear or uncertainty, who knew beyond any doubt that this one man—this proud, strong, gentle man—was the one man she wanted for all time.

He believed in truth and he fought for justice. He was tough, wary of involvements, highly selective but he made her think and laugh and trust. The first time she'd seen him, he'd scared her. She'd known right then that she wouldn't be able to ignore what he made her feel. She was going to have to deal with it head-on, no holds barred. Right now.

He was a good six inches taller than her. She had to reach up to twine her arms around his neck and bring his head down to hers. For an instant she saw the hesitation in his eyes and the concern. He was worried about her. The knowledge of that wiped out any fear she might have felt. Her lips touched his once, twice, tentatively. A low growl broke from him. His arms tightened around her. A big hand cupped the back of her head, holding her in place. His mouth took hers consumingly, commanding the response she was fully ready to give.

Chapter 12

Flynn's hands moved along Constance's flanks, stroking the soft, heated skin. She moaned faintly. They were in his bed at the back of the house where he had carried her. Neither remembered getting there, not that it mattered. Both were naked, their few clothes discarded on the floor. The storm outside still raged, but they were oblivious to it, caught as they were in the far greater storm of their own making.

"Beautiful," he murmured thickly. In the dim light his face looked cast in stone, the planes and hollows thrown into sharp relief. His skin appeared bronzed. The powerful muscles of his arms and shoulders clenched as he moved.

Constance's back arched, bringing her breasts closer to the seeking warmth of his mouth. His tongue stroked the soft undersides, drifting slowly upward, drawing in a circular motion around each straining nipple. When she could bear it no longer, she grasped the thick mane of his hair and drew him to her.

He suckled her urgently, drawing her almost completely into his mouth. She cried out, her hips rising and falling against him as the pulsing heat within threatened to become unbearable.

He drew back slightly and looked down at her. Her auburn hair spread over the pillow in tumbled disarray. Her lips were swollen from the roughness of his kisses, and her eyes were heavy with the passion that gripped them both. A soft flush caused by the abrasion of his unshaven cheeks spread across the tender flesh he had just caressed.

He touched his tongue to her again, laving the slight redness, drifting into the cleft between her breasts, farther down along her concave stomach and the tiny pillow of her abdomen stretched almost taut between her hips. She whispered his name convulsively. He smiled against her skin and was swept by a wave of tenderness such as he had never known. Passion, yes, for he was a passionate man and no stranger to the driving need to possess a woman, though he kept it in strict-enough check most of the time. But this was different. Wanting her didn't begin to describe what he felt. He was struck by the sudden awareness that he needed this woman, needed the sweet strength of her body and mind more than he had ever needed anything. The realization filled him with a piercing sense of his own vulnerability. For an instant he almost drew back.

Her hands stopped him, strong and slender, reaching out to claim him in the most elemental way possible. "No more," she murmured, "please... now..."

A low growl broke from him. He slid his hands beneath her buttocks and lifted her to him. Then he was within her, driving hard and deep, unable any longer to restrain the overwhelming, insistent hunger that threatened to consume him.

Constance welcomed him with every fiber of her being. Each long, penetrating stroke brought her closer and closer to the shimmering heat radiating through her. She raised her hips, meeting him fully. The powerful inner muscles of her body worked, holding and releasing, holding and releasing. He cried out hoarsely, and for the first time she felt the full unleashing of his strength as the last shreds of control slipped from him. Far in the back of her mind she knew she should be afraid, but fear was beyond her. They were one, moving together toward an incandescent light that, when it burst upon them, hurtled them both into a world that for a brief, eternal moment was purely their own.

Afterward they rested, her head pillowed on his chest, as their heartbeats slowly returned to normal. Flynn touched her hair gently, breathing in the scent of her perfume that clung to her skin, and beneath it, the deeper, muskier scent of sheer womanliness. He smiled faintly in the darkness. She saw and smiled herself, tentatively.

"What's so funny?" she asked.

He looked down, meeting her eyes. "Funny? Nothing at all. More like ironic."

"Why do you say that?"

"Only that being a man who always prided himself on a certain amount of self-discipline, I've had a rude awakening to reality."

Her smile deepened. She laughed softly. "Oh, that, it's good for you."

His hands tightened in gentle warning. "A woman of the world talking, I suppose?"

"No," she answered in all honesty, "I was never that, but I do know there are some things you just can't fight. For better or worse, you and I have run smack into one of them."

"And which one would that be?" he murmured, his eyes darkening to the glint of gold. "Sex? Passion? Or maybe simple gratitude at being alive?"

The words stung. She had been thinking about something that went far beyond any of that. Alive, he had said, as in not dead. Dead...Sheffield...the whole stinking mess. Just when she had been closest to forgetting it, if only temporarily, he flung it right back at her.

Damn the man. He had no right to do this, not when she was so completely fulfilled beyond her wildest dreams, so relaxed, so ready to slip into a dreamless sleep. He had to go asking questions that didn't have any answers, at least none she was ready to deal with.

"Take it easy," he murmured, sensing the sudden tension in her. He should have been more sensitive to her feelings or more honest about his own. But that was hindsight, and right now what he needed was damage control.

"This is all new to me," he said softly, turning over so that she was beneath him, glaring like an azure-eyed cat and all the more delicious for it. "It's going to take work to get it right," he added. "But that's okay, I'm a patient man."

Also an infuriating one if he thought she was going to make it that easy for him. "It's nothing," she said, turning her head away. "Just sex, like you said."

He uttered an expletive and came down on her hard. She eluded his grasp, slid across the bed and glared at him. He almost followed but instead fell back suddenly against the pillows and sighed.

"I'm sorry, I should be doing better than this, but the truth is I'm not quite myself at the moment."

Despite herself, the corners of her mouth twitched upward. He looked so truly contrite that she couldn't help but relent, if only a little.

"Who are you, then?"

"Just some poor exhausted male, confused to the depths of his being, who's just found out what it's like to fall headfirst off a cliff."

"You're full of blarney, you know that?"

"Of course I do. It's in the genes. You can't blame me for that."

"Hmm, we'll see. If you're so tired, why don't you go to sleep?"

"Ah, well, actually, I seem to have something else on my mind."

Her gaze wandered over the unabashedly magnificent length of his body, her eyes widening. "Poor exhausted male, my foot."

"And a lovely foot it is, give it here."

"No, Flynn, absolutely not."

Lighting cracked above them. He ignored it and reached for her. His hand slid down her leg, around the slender calf, to grasp a slim ankle. Holding her captive, he deliberately ran a finger up along the bottom of her foot.

"That tickles! Stop!"

"Make me."

Again the quick, teasing caress, again the burst of half foolish, half sensual pleasure.

"Stop!"

"I told you, you have to make me."

"And how am I supposed to do that, you rat?"

His teeth gleamed whitely in the darkness. "You could distract me."

She breathed in sharply, taking his meaning. "That sounds like a challenge."

"Any reason why not?"

"Only that you might get more than you're bargaining for," she said, fighting the wave of excitement rising within her. This teasing, provocative Flynn was a new experience. He filled her with a sense of her own power and the eagerness to test it.

She moved slowly at first, with a certain tentativeness that gave way quickly enough as he groaned beneath her. "Don't stop," he murmured.

She didn't, not until they were both deep into the light once again, caught in the convulsive waves of pleasure that shattered all barriers and left them truly as one.

Much later Flynn stirred lazily beside her. "I was just thinking," he said.

"Oh, no, I failed. His brain still works."

He chuckled softly. "Only tiny parts of it. Anyway, what I was thinking was that I may have to change my opinion of thunderstorms. Maybe they're not so bad after all."

"Or maybe you just found something useful to do while they're going on."

"There is that," he agreed. "We could wait for the next storm and test it out."

"Why wait?" Constance murmured.

"I'm beginning to get the feeling that I'm in big trouble," Flynn said, not sounding as though he minded very much.

"How big?" she asked, and sat up slightly, holding her hands apart. "This big . . . or this . . . ?"

Flynn shook his head in mock dismay. "And you such a nice girl."

"Oh, well, if you'd rather not . . ."

"Big," Flynn said, "definitely big." And drew her to him.

He awoke to a room flooded by light and the fresh-washed scent of rain come and gone. For a time he lay unmoving, still and quiet within himself. The bed beside him was empty, but the sheets were still warm and the pillow bore the imprint of where Constance had lain. He touched it gently, touching as he did the images still swirling through his mind.

He had dreamed chaotically, vivid images in color scattering across the landscape of his subconscious. He closed his eyes for a moment, trying to recall them, but he could remember only Constance—beautiful and seductive—and incongruously, Elizabeth Sheffield, her head nodding like a china doll's as she listened to the praises of her son.

He got out of bed quickly and went into the bathroom, turning on the shower. While it was still cold he stepped under and let the icy water pummel him

When he'd had enough, he got out, wrapped himself in a white terry-cloth robe and shaved. Back in the bedroom he put on crisp khaki trousers and a conservative "Black Watch" plaid shirt. He slung a russet corduroy jacket over his shoulder and headed for the kitchen.

It was empty, but nearby he heard the shower running in the guest room. He hung the jacket over the back of a chair and got to work. Constance found him there a little while later, drawn by the scent of coffee and the sizzle of bacon. He didn't see her for a moment, giving her the chance to study him unobserved. He looked very large standing in front of the counter wielding a fork as he beat eggs. His broad shoulders strained the soft, dark shirt he wore. His waist and hips were lean, his thighs heavily muscled even through the khaki slacks. His ebony hair was still slightly damp. It curled slightly at the nape of his neck. She resisted the impulse to reach out to touch him and instead cleared her throat.

"Good morning," she said.

He turned, startled by how quietly she had approached. His eyes swept over her. She was dressed in a plain wool skirt whose soft blue shade complimented her eyes. With it she wore a pale mauve sweater. The delicacy of the colors emphasized the vividness of her hair swept back from her face and secured with tortoiseshell combs. He had never seen anything so beautiful—plain and simple. She filled him with a bewildering mixture of fierce desire and overwhelming tenderness. Beside her, everything else—the case, the world, everything—was eclipsed.

"Good morning," he said. "Did you sleep well?"

The question made her flush, reminding her as it did of the intimacies that had finally led to mutual exhaustion. Fighting down her self-consciousness she nodded. "And you?"

"Fine." He gestured to the food. "I hope you're hungry."

His cool tone left her confused. Obviously he didn't care to dwell on what had happened during the night. Just as obviously, she was going to have to match his coolness, if only for the sake of her pride. "Starving," she said as blithely as she could manage. "What can I do to help?"

"You can set the table. Everything's over there." He gestured toward a large oak cabinet set along one wall before turning his attention back to the stove.

She laid out plates and cutlery on the table while he folded the beaten eggs into omelets lightly flavored with herbs. Along with them came coffee, croissants and a selection of jams.

Constance took a bite of the omelet and looked at him in surprise. "You're a good cook."

"Don't be so shocked. It doesn't take a genius."

"It's still unusual, at least for men." She glanced around at the amply laden table, the cheerful, efficient kitchen, and was struck by the care that had gone into it. "Are you always so well prepared for unexpected guests?"

He shook his head. "I don't have guests up here. The terrible truth is that I tend to pamper myself."

No guests. No women. That cheered her immensely. Okay, maybe she was being just a tiny bit immature, but what the heck. "There's nothing wrong with that," she said as she spread a spoonful of marmalade on a croissant. "Are we still going to the school today?"

Flynn nodded. He was relieved to have the conversation turn to business. Later they'd have to talk about other things, but for the moment he was glad to be back on more familiar ground. "I haven't been in touch with the headmaster's office, so there's a chance he'll be out. But I think it's worth taking the risk to catch him off guard."

"Lewis was only there for a year. He may not remember much about him."

"Maybe not. We'll find out. Would you like more coffee?"

She shook her head. Across the table their eyes met. Without warning, hardly aware herself of what she was going to say, she asked, "Do you always take such good care of your clients, I mean personally?"

He flushed slightly. "If you mean do I sleep with them, no, I most definitely do not."

"I didn't mean that. I meant the rest, the attention, the genuine concern."

He looked at her directly. "No, I don't."

In for a penny—she'd gone this far, she might as well keep going. "Why are you doing so now?"

The question hung between them, demanding an answer. Flynn put his fork down slowly. His manner grew very quiet. The confusion he'd been feeling within himself died away, leaving only simple truth. "Because," he said, "you were right about what you said last night, about there being some things you can't fight. I think I'm falling in love with you."

Constance inhaled sharply. She felt the rush of warmth to her cheeks and wished desperately that she was more adept at concealing her feelings.

"Oh..."

"Yeah, oh."

She cleared her throat, gripped her courage and plunged. "Yes, well, actually the same thing seems to be happening to me."

"Oh."

They grinned at each other across the table. Sunlight flooded the room. Outside, birds were singing, and a soft, fragrant breeze fluttered the new-born leaves. It was one of those moments when life reveals its capacity for being absolutely perfect.

If it had been a movie, the camera would have panned back and done a slow fade-out. But this was real life, which meant the perfect moments never lingered very long, except when they were wrapped away in memory. Real life—confusing, difficult, sometimes painful—went marching on.

"I guess we'd better be going soon," Flynn said.

"I guess..."

"Constance..."

She drew back slightly, looking at him. "Later might be better, when this is all over."

He met her gaze. Slowly he nodded. "Later."

Chapter 13

The plaque on the high stone wall read Hawkins School. Next to it a double wrought-iron gate stood open. A gravel driveway lined by old oak trees led out of sight. To one side was a large, pristine lake on which several swans floated lazily. To the other were emerald playing fields dotted by soccer goals.

"Nice place," Flynn said. "Just like the high school I went to in Hoboken."

"Oh, yes?" Constance asked. She had relaxed some in the drive from the cabin. The shock of what had happened between them certainly hadn't worn off but it had settled in somewhat. Underneath it, just starting to bubble up, she could feel the potential for a happiness so enormous it almost frightened her. Especially when she considered that it might never remain more than a possibility unless fortune chose to smile on them spectacularly. Not caring to calculate the odds of that happening, she turned her mind to other things. The Hawkins School, for instance, and the young Lewis Sheffield who had briefly attended it.

"Yeah," Flynn said. "We had air, dirt, even some grass right in front behind the steel mesh fence. Of course, it wasn't the same color grass as here. You know the old one about how to get lawns like this?"

Constance shook her head. She leaned back in the seat and made a deliberate decision to enjoy herself. Why not? Either they'd find something out from the headmaster or they wouldn't. Either they'd convince the D.A. not to prosecute or they wouldn't. Either her life would work out or it wouldn't. As Howard Bartlett had said, life just keeps marching on no matter what you thought, so you might as well snatch some fun along the way.

"Seed, water, fertilize and roll for a hundred years," Flynn said.

"Sounds about right. How long has Hawkins been here?"

"Founded 1820."

"How did you know that?" she asked.

"It's a little embarrassing...."

"Oh, good, tell me."

He shot her a chiding glance but complied. "One of my first cases right after I joined the bar took me up against a hotshot assistant D.A. that everyone said would cream me. Even my own client figured I didn't have a chance, which meant he didn't. I was dumb enough to believe we could win but the A.D.A.— that's assistant district attorney, by the way—had everybody psyched. He was one of those have-it-all types, right family, right schools, right tie, everything. Anyway, I set out to learn everything I could about him, figuring there had to be a chink in the armor somewhere. To make a long story longer, it turned out he went to Hawkins, which is how I happened to learn about the place including when it was founded.''

"How many years ago was that?'' Constance asked.

"I told you, 1820.''

"No, how many years since you went up against that guy?''

"Twelve, thirteen. Why?''

"After all that time, you still remembered a little detail like when the prep school he went to was founded?''

Flynn grinned lopsidedly. "Scary, isn't it?''

"Petrifying. Are you always like that?''

He nodded. "I have a real hard time forgetting anything.''

"So what happened, did you find the chink?''

"No, I didn't. It turned out that he was such a hotshot because he was damn good.''

"You lost?'' Constance asked.

"Nope, I won. He was good, but I was better.'' There was unmistakable satisfaction in that. Early on Flynn had tested himself against the big guys and come out on top. No wonder he'd let nothing stand in his way since.

And no wonder he enjoyed going head-to-head with people like the Sheffields.

The gravel driveway turned a corner. Directly ahead was a massive redbrick building garlanded with ivy. White columns rose around the portico entrance. The scent of newly mown grass was strong on the air. Off in the distance, from somewhere within the building, came the sterling sound of young male voices raised in song.

"It's like a movie set," Constance murmured as she got out of the car. Gardenias bloomed in pots beside the entrance. Nearby, perfectly shaped magnolias were coming into flower. Everywhere she looked every small detail was perfection itself.

Inside was no different. The main entrance led to a marbled hall that smelled of beeswax and lemon polish. A large, winding staircase led to the upper reaches of the building. Along its length and throughout the hall were elaborately framed paintings. Some depicted the school itself while others were of the long and distinguished line of headmasters who had led it.

A boy appeared at the top of the stairs. He was dressed in khaki shorts and a striped rugby shirt. A lacrosse stick was balanced on his shoulder. Shin guards covered most of his legs. He came hurtling down the steps with the unbridled urgency of youth. When he saw them he halted.

Cautiously he asked, "May I help you?"

"We're looking for the headmaster," Flynn said. "Would you know where we could find him?"

"Dr. Harrison is in the conservatory, sir."

"Thank you, and where would that be?"

The boy gave directions before rushing off. They followed his directions through the east wing of the building to the back, where a connecting passage led to a large, Victorian-style greenhouse. Within was a lush, almost steamy tropical paradise festooned by tall trees and flowering bushes. No one seemed to be about except for a tall, slender man bent over a tray of orchids.

"Excuse me," Flynn said.

The man started. He dropped the tweezers he had been using to exchange pollen from one flower to the other and stared at them.

"Yes?" he said.

"Are you Dr. Harrison?" Flynn asked. The man was in his midfifties with thinning blond hair, aquiline features and an air of perpetual distraction. He was clearly not pleased to have his privacy invaded but would not be so rude as to actually say so.

"I am. You are?"

"Flynn Corbett. This is Miss Constance Lehane. We'd like a few minutes of your time if you wouldn't mind."

The headmaster hesitated. A glimmer of recognition moved in his face when Flynn said their names. "I don't recall that we had an appointment."

"We don't, but the matter is urgent."

Again the man hesitated. With palpable reluctance he removed the thin leather work gloves he was wearing and tossed them onto the tray. "Very well, then, come along. But I have little time to spare."

"This won't take long," Flynn assured him.

Harrison showed them into a ground-floor office paneled in mahogany and furnished with the usual chintz and hunting-print style popular in English country homes. He indicated seats in front of a burled chestnut desk. Taking his own chair, with the desk between them, he said, "Now, what is it you want?"

"We'd like to talk with you about Lewis Sheffield. He was a pupil here in 1971. Were you at the school then?"

Grudgingly Harrison nodded. "I was on the faculty."

"Do you remember Lewis?"

"Not very well. His older brother, Charles, had been here and done quite well. But as you undoubtedly know, Lewis's tenure was brief. That happens sometimes. Not every school is for every boy. At any rate, he moved on after about a year."

"While he was here, how did he do?" Constance asked softly.

Harrison cast her a quelling glance. "You can hardly expect me to discuss the performance of a pupil with strangers, Miss Lehane. That would hardly be proper."

"We're not asking you to do that," Flynn interposed quickly. "We're merely trying to get some idea of his character. Was he cooperative, well behaved, that sort of thing?"

"Yes."

"I see . . . there were no problems?"

"I didn't say that. Almost every boy has problems of some sort. Lewis was not exceptional."

"Then why did he leave?" Constance asked.

"I told you, sometimes a boy simply does better in a different environment. Perhaps Lewis felt overshadowed by his older brother, who knows? At any rate, he was here only a short time and he went on to other things. That's all."

"Nothing precipitated his departure?" Flynn asked. He leaned forward slightly, staring at the headmaster. "There was no . . . incident, for example?"

A shadow moved behind Harrison's eyes. It was so quick that it could easily have been missed, but Constance was sure it had happened. So was Flynn. He smiled imperceptibly.

"I have no idea what you mean," the headmaster asserted. "Lewis Sheffield was a perfectly ordinary boy. Now, if there is nothing else—" He stood up, indicating that the meeting was over.

Flynn also rose and Constance after him, but they made no immediate move to leave. "How many boys would you say have gone through this school in the years you've been here?" Flynn asked.

"Perhaps ten thousand," Harrison replied. He drummed his fingers on the desk impatiently.

"Of all those, how many have left after a year for no particular cause?"

"I have no idea. I really must be going."

Flynn relented, or at least he appeared to. He thanked Harrison for his assistance and took Constance's arm. Together they left the office and the building.

Outside in the sunlight she said, "So much for that." Despite the clear, balmy day, depression threatened. Maybe it hadn't been realistic, but she'd been hoping they'd come away with something, anything to indicate that she was telling the truth. Instead, they had yet another picture-postcard view of Lewis Sheffield, Mr. Straight Arrow.

"It's okay," Flynn said gently. He opened the car door for her. "You must still be tired. Didn't you notice how weird all that was?"

She waited until he was behind the wheel before responding. "Kind of, but so what? He said Lewis was at the school, he left for no special reason, and that's that. We got nothing."

Flynn shook his head. He smiled as he gunned the motor. His eyes held an unmistakable look of satisfaction. "It wasn't what Harrison said. It was what he didn't say. He never asked us what we were doing there. Two people, strangers, come waltzing in to ask questions about some kid who was at the school twenty years ago, and he doesn't wonder why."

"He knew who we were," Constance said slowly. She had sensed that for herself, but the implications hadn't sunk in until now. Almost to herself she said, "He was prepared for us."

"Bingo. We had no appointment but we were expected. Maybe not today necessarily, but sometime relatively soon. Harrison wasn't surprised at all when we turned up. He's not a very good actor and he's uncomfortable lying, but he did the best that he could. He stonewalled us."

"By claiming there was nothing unusual about Lewis."

"Right. He even claimed he had no idea how many boys left the school without graduating. That's baloney. A headmaster would have that at his fingertips."

"All right," she said slowly, "but where does that get us? We still don't know anything."

"No, but I'm convinced now that we're in the right place. Something did happen twenty years ago to cause Lewis's departure from Hawkins. Given his family's priorities, how much they would have wanted and expected him to finish here, it would have had to be something fairly big. They're still trying to keep it hushed up.''

"I don't know," Constance said slowly. "I want to believe you, but there's nothing to go on. Maybe Harrison has stomach problems or something. Maybe that's why he acted the way he did. We could be going completely in the wrong direction.''

"We could," Flynn agreed, "but there are times when you have to go with your instincts. I need to stop for some gas. You want anything?''

"I could use another cup of coffee," Constance admitted. Also a chance to powder her nose and gather her thoughts. The interview with Harrison had shaken her more than she wanted to admit. What if Flynn was wrong? What if there really wasn't anything to discover about Lewis?

Stop that, the little voice in the back of her mind said. Just stop. Take it one step at a time, and everything will work out all right.

Smart, that little voice, but then it was safe down inside her somewhere while she was out there on the front line trying to cope.

"Definitely coffee," she said.

They pulled up in front of a diner that had a gas station next door. While Flynn got the tank filled, Constance stopped by the ladies' room. When she came out, he was seated at a booth waiting for her.

He stood up as she approached. The old-fashioned allantry touched Constance. With some men she might have suspected it was contrived, but with Flynn she knew the instinct to courtesy ran deep.

"Thank you," she murmured when he offered her a menu, "but after that breakfast, I couldn't eat a bite." She looked up at the waitress. "Just coffee, please."

Flynn asked for the same. After the waitress left, he said, "We've got to lay out some strategy. I think the best thing is for you to stay here for a few days while I head back to New York and see what I can dig up on Lewis's old school chums."

"Where do you start? The school certainly won't cooperate."

"Remember the A.D.A. I told you about? He runs a private practice out in Seattle now. He would have been a few years ahead of Lewis, but I'm going to give him a call. It's worth a try to see what might turn up."

Constance nodded. She had no illusions about what he'd just told her. It was a very slim lead that could easily peter out, but at least it was something.

"What about—?" she began only to break off as the waitress returned with their coffee. The woman set the cups in front of them but instead of leaving she hesitated, staring down at them.

"Would you like anything else?" she asked.

"No, thanks," Flynn replied.

Still, the woman didn't move. She glanced from one of them to the other. Her lower lip was caught between her teeth. She raised a hand nervously to smooth short blond hair. Constance guessed she was in her midthirties. There were a few fine lines around her eyes, but otherwise her face was smooth and a tractive. She was tall with a good figure and an air of competence overlaid by unexplained anxiousness.

"Is something wrong?" Constance asked.

The woman glanced over her shoulder at the burly man working behind the counter. He was deep in conversation with a couple of truckers who had just come in. Softly, her voice little more than a whisper, she asked, "Are you that woman from New York the paper said was involved in Lewis Sheffield's death?"

It was Constance's turn to hesitate. She glanced at Flynn quickly. He remained silent, sitting back in the booth.

"He died in my apartment," she admitted.

The woman turned her gaze on Flynn. "Who are you?"

"I'm her attorney. My name's Flynn Corbett."

The woman nodded. "You're here because of the school, aren't you?"

"That's right," Flynn said. "We just came from there. But how did you know that?"

The woman didn't answer directly. Instead, she said, "I'll bet you didn't get much. They really know how to close ranks."

Flynn and Constance exchanged a quick look. Her pulse beat more quickly. She pulled her hands off the table and put them in her lap where no one could see that they were tightly clenched.

Softly Flynn said, "That's for sure. It seemed like they barely remembered Lewis. But maybe that's not true of everyone around here...." He let the suggestion trail off, leaving it to the woman to decide.

She stared back at him, revealing nothing. Only the strained look in her eyes hinted at her anxiety. The man behind the counter glanced their way. "The apple pie's good," the woman said, raising her voice slightly. "You can have it à la mode or with cheddar cheese."

Flynn shook his head. "No, thanks, coffee's fine."

She shrugged and handed them the check. "Suit yourself."

A moment later she was gone, disappearing into the back of the diner. Constance almost stood up to go after her, but Flynn put his hand on her arm quickly.

"Sit down," he ordered.

"Why? Maybe there's something she could tell us...."

"She's spooked," Flynn said. "You go after her now, and she won't tell you a thing. Later—"

"I'm sick of later."

"Too bad." His voice held a note of harshness. "I'm not crazy about it myself but I know there are times when you have to wait no matter how tough it is. I'll find out who she is, we'll track her down, and if she has anything to say, we'll get it."

Constance slumped back in the seat. Her composure, strained as it was, threatened to crack. "Oh, God," she murmured, "I hope so."

Flynn reached out again and took her hand. "Come on, you've gotten this far. Don't give up now."

His strength and the warmth of his touch reached her. She lifted her head and managed a wan smile. "Sure thing, Sir Flynn."

"Good girl. Finish your coffee and we'll go." He picked up the check and turned it over. A great stillness settled over him.

"What is it?" Constance murmured.

He held the check out silently so that she could read what was written there below their order. The words were scribbled in pale pencil but still clearly legible.

Christine LeMoix. 134 Decateur St. 8:00 p.m.

Chapter 14

Number 134 Decateur Street was a narrow, clap-
board row house half a dozen blocks away from the
diner. It was part of a collection of such houses built
for the employees of a now-defunct piano factory that
had once flourished in the region. Over the years many
of the houses had fallen into disrepair, their roofs
missing shingles, shutters coming loose and their yards
becoming overgrown. Number 134 was the exception. It was freshly painted, the grass cut and everything about it exactly as it should be.

Flynn rang the bell, then stood back slightly and
waited. A moment passed before he and Constance
heard footsteps. The man who opened the door was in
his forties, tall and heavyset and dressed in work
clothes. He looked like he might drive a truck for a
living or perhaps handle one of the scattering of boats
that still ran goods up and down the nearby river.

"You Corbett?" he demanded.

Flynn nodded cordially. "That's me. This is Miss Lehane. Is Mrs. LeMoix here?"

The man continued to stare at him for a moment before abruptly coming to some decision within himself. "Yeah, she's here." He thrust out his hand. "I'm Patrick LeMoix. Chrissie's my wife."

"It's good of you to see us," Constance said softly.

The man shrugged. "It's not my doing. When she read about you in the paper and said she wanted to go down to New York to talk to you, I told her she was nuts. But what with you turning up here and her having a chance to think about things..." He made a gesture of resignation, if not acceptance. "I guess this is just something she has to do."

Before either Flynn or Constance could reply, a woman's voice called from the back of the house. "Bring them in here, Patrick. They're not going to stand around in the hall all night."

The big man sighed but did as he was bidden. He led the way down a narrow hall that gave way to a large, bright kitchen. Christine LeMoix was sitting at the table. She stood up when they entered.

"Hi," she said shyly, looking from one to the other. She still had on her waitressing uniform and she appeared tired, but there was an edge of determination in her eyes that couldn't be missed.

"Sit down, why don't you. I'll get you a drink. Coffee, maybe?"

"A drink would be good," Flynn said casually. "You got a beer?"

"Yeah, sure," Patrick LeMoix said. He waved his wife back into her chair and headed for the fridge. "How about you, miss?"

"Beer will be fine," Constance said.

He cracked the tops on three bottles and handed them around. "Okay," he said as he took his seat, "so you're here. Before you ask Chrissie any questions, I want to get a few ground rules straight."

"Pat..." his wife began only to be brushed off gently but firmly.

"First things first, honey. I know what you have to say is important but I want to make sure you don't end up regretting it." He looked at Flynn hard. "I wouldn't take kindly to you blabbing around what she's about to tell you. This is a small town and people can get hurt. You understand?"

"I think so," Flynn said slowly. "If Mrs. Le-Moix—"

"Please, call me Chrissie."

"Thank you, Chrissie. If she's going to say what I think she is, it's only natural that she'd want it dealt with as discreetly as possible. However, for the information to be useful to us, I need to—"

"How do you know what I'm going to say?" Chrissie asked, her eyes dark. "I've never breathed a word of it to anyone except Pat here. You can't know—"

"I know Lewis Sheffield," Flynn explained gently. "At least I'm starting to. I said all along that this incident with Constance could be explained in only two ways. Either Sheffield suddenly behaved in an entirely different manner from anything he'd ever done before, or he'd been involved in other attacks or women. And the more I learn about him, the more I experience the cover-up his family is trying to engineer, the more convinced I am that it's the latter."

There was silence for a moment before Chrissie suddenly lowered her head. In a strained voice she said, "I knew it. All these years I knew I couldn't have been the only one. I used to lie awake wondering if he was doing it to someone else. But I was so damn young and my family—"

"What about your family?" Constance asked gently. Her throat was tight. For the present her own situation didn't seem so important. She was looking into the face of a woman who had suffered more than herself and endured it in silence for years.

"They made me keep quiet," Chrissie said. She reached into the pocket of her apron for a crumpled tissue and pressed it to her eyes. "I was thirteen years old, just a kid. What choice did I have?"

"There was nothing she could do," her husband said harshly. "Her father'd been laid off from his job six months before—they were up to their ears in debt. Along came the Sheffields, flashing a big check and promising that if they didn't take it, if they tried to make any trouble, they'd regret it for the rest of their lives."

"They took the money," Constance said. The thought horrified her, but so did the need that had made it seem like the only alternative. She'd been lucky herself, growing up in a solid, stable family where the hard times never really hit. Flynn was different. He'd known what it was like to be poor and the look on his face said he understood what Chrissie eMoix's people had gone through.

"What exactly happened to you?" Flynn asked softly.

"I was taking a shortcut behind the school," she said. "It was a nice day, warm, bright, I didn't think anything of it. At least not until Lewis Sheffield popped up out of the bushes. I'd seen him before a few times in town. I thought he was a real snot, arrogant and just plain mean. All the townie kids were told to keep their distance from the Hawkins' bunch. We didn't always listen, but everyone knew to give Lewis a wide berth."

"What did you do?" Flynn continued.

"I tried to go around him, but he wouldn't let me. He kept jumping in front of me, blocking the path. He was taunting me, you see. I thought he just wanted to scare me but then I found out I was wrong."

Her voice broke, but she kept going anyway, needing after so long to get it out once and for all. "He knocked me down and dragged me back behind some rocks. I really fought him, trying to get away, I swear to God I did, but he was too strong. He…he did what he wanted to, and then he let me go. He told me to keep my mouth shut or there'd be trouble." Her face pale, hands tightly clenched, she said, "He was laughing. I'll always remember that, the way he laughed."

Patrick LeMoix got up and went to stand behind his wife. He put a hand on her shoulder. He looked very grim. "He's not laughing now, he's dead. But it's not right what the family's trying to pull. We've heard it on TV." He looked at Constance. "How they're saying he was some kind of saint and you killed him. That's a crock, plain and simple."

"What did your family do after they found out what happened?" Flynn asked.

"My father went to the headmaster and the headmaster called the Sheffields. They pulled Lewis out of the school immediately and sent him off somewhere. They were allowed to do that, the school let them, even though they knew the police should have talked to him. All any of them cared about was keeping him out of trouble and shutting me up."

"That's all they still care about," Flynn said, "only in this case, they couldn't keep Miss Lehane quiet. She told the police immediately that Sheffield had attacked her. Once that was on the record, all the family could do was try to destroy her reputation."

"Don't let them," Chrissie said, almost pleading. "Somebody's got to win against them even though Lewis is dead. They've got to learn they can't always have things their way."

"I agree," Flynn said, "but in order to do that I need your permission to tell what happened to you to a few people."

"Like who?" Patrick demanded.

"Like the district attorney on the case, Ben Morgenstern. He's got to know that the incident with Constance wasn't the first. That will have a bearing on whether or not he takes this to the grand jury."

"I don't want to have to testify in front of any jury," Chrissie said quickly.

"Grand jury proceedings aren't like regular trials," Flynn said soothingly. "They're closed, which means whatever goes on in them is kept confidential. But I don't think you'd be called under any circumstances. Our goal is to get the case against Constance dropped completely."

"I'm for that," Patrick said. "Okay, tell this Morgenstern guy, just make sure it doesn't get back here. Chrissie's got a right to walk around this town without people whispering behind her back."

Constance thought of what people had been saying about her and nodded emphatically. "You have my word, Mrs. LeMoix. What you've told us will be treated with kid gloves. You've been through more than enough. I really appreciate your having the courage to help me."

"That's all right," Chrissie said softly. "It didn't really take any courage. I guess I'm still so angry about what happened." She shrugged. "Anyway, I just hope it will be enough."

"So do I," Flynn murmured. The way he said it suggested he was far from convinced.

"What do you think?" Constance asked later after they had left the house and were walking back toward the car. It was getting on ten o'clock. They'd stayed, chatting with the LeMoixes about more pleasant matters. Flynn, as usual, got into a deep conversation with Patrick about life in small Connecticut towns, working on the river—it turned out Patrick did run a boat—and what the Bruins were likely to do. Constance talked with Chrissie about the couple's children; they had two who were away visiting relatives. The way she spoke of them, the gentle love and pride in her voice, brought a lump to Constance's throat. She thought of herself, the elegant apartment, the big job, and wondered why it all didn't seem to mean much anymore.

"What do I think?" Flynn repeated slowly. He'd been unusually quiet since leaving the row house. His thoughts threatened to absorb him. "I think we've made some progress," he said. "I'll get on the horn to Morgenstern first thing in the morning. The trouble is it's just one person and it was a long time ago at that."

"He raped her," Constance exclaimed. "She was thirteen years old and he raped her. How can that not make a difference?"

"He was fourteen years old," Flynn reminded her. "A minor in the eyes of the law. If her family had tried to pursue the case, he'd have been tried as a juvie and walked with maybe a couple of months in some fancy rest home his family paid for. Besides, he was never charged, let alone convicted. Ben will have to take all of that into consideration."

"I don't believe this. It sounds like you're telling me he got away with it then and he's going to get away with it now!"

"Not exactly," Flynn said quietly. "As Patrick pointed out, he is dead."

Constance swallowed hard. For one horrible moment she'd actually forgotten that Lewis Sheffield was no longer alive. He threatened to haunt her as much as he had Chrissie.

"Okay, he's dead, but at the moment that's not helping me much."

"I'll talk to Morgenstern," Flynn said again. "This is important—it will influence his thinking, but I can't guarantee that it will be enough."

"What *will* be?" Constance asked.

"I don't know," he said honestly. Under his breath he added, "I wish I did."

They drove back to the cabin in silence. Constance stared out the window at the darkness. The events of the past few days had left her drained. She felt as though she'd been on a roller coaster alternating between valleys of despair and peaks of exultation.

Sitting next to Flynn in the car, closed in by the night, she wished she had nothing on her mind except being with him. How lovely it would be to drive along the country road under the stars to the secluded cabin where nothing would prevent the full expression of their feelings for each other. But despite what they had already shared, something did stand in the way.

The night before, when there had been only the hope of discovery, she had been able to put everything aside at least for a time. But now that the hope was realized yet still might not be enough, it was almost more than she could bear.

"I'm so tired," she murmured.

"What was that?" Flynn asked.

Constance shook her head. She hardly realized she'd spoken out loud. "Nothing, just that I could use some sleep."

He cast her a quick look, taking in the shadows beneath her eyes, the lines of strain around her mouth and the slight slump to her shoulders. Gently he said, "Then that's what you'll get."

She nodded, torn between relief and disappointment. He was a good man, he understood. But in the end she felt very much on her own. She'd curl up in the guest bed under all the covers and try to convince herself that everything would be all right.

Except Flynn had other ideas. When he had parked the car, he got out and opened the passenger door. Before she could object, he lifted her from the seat and strode with her toward the cabin.

"Flynn, what are you doing?" she demanded.

Moonlight caught the utter masculinity of his smile. "Putting you to bed, what else?"

"You don't have to..."

"Shh, relax. Let me take care of it, okay?"

Was there a woman anywhere who could resist such a request? Constance certainly wasn't up to it. The temptation to relax back in his arms overwhelmed her. She let her eyes droop shut and felt beneath her cheek the soothing beat of his heart.

He carried her through the front door and into the entry hall, but instead of going up the steps to the guest room, he continued on toward the back of the house and the master bedroom. Constance protested halfheartedly but she was genuinely too tired as well as too content to make much of an objection.

By the time he laid her down on the wide bed she was almost asleep. She came awake as she felt him gently undoing the waistband of her slacks.

"What are you—?" she began.

"Just getting you comfortable."

Hard to argue with that, she thought hazily. Especially when his hands were so warm and strong, moving over her deftly until everything was removed except the lacy bra and panties she had put on that morning.

There he stopped, and stood in the moonlight looking down at her. The silvered light made her skin look like ivory. Banked fires glowed in her hair.

Through the thin fabric of her lingerie, he could see the ruby contours of her nipples and the dark shadow between her thighs.

His breath deepened, growing harsher. "So beautiful," he murmured.

"Mmm."

Flynn grinned wryly to himself. Some big seduction scene, but then he hadn't expected otherwise. She was entitled to be worn-out. She'd been through a hell of a time and it wasn't over yet. But it could be interrupted at least for a few hours. For that brief time he would see to it that she rested.

Ignoring the clamoring demands of his own body, he pulled the blankets back, slipped her into the bed and settled the covers in place. When he was done, he sat down quietly on the edge of the bed and looked at her. She was deeply asleep. The shadows were still under her eyes, but otherwise she looked far more relaxed than she had in the car. He could find some satisfaction in that, for whatever it was worth.

He went into the bathroom and stripped off his clothes. Standing under the shower, he thought about what he would say to Morgenstern. From there his mind drifted to Lewis Sheffield. A wave of disgust washed over him. Ben might distrust Chrissie LeMoix's story but he hadn't seen and heard her. Flynn was dead sure she was telling the truth. At fourteen Sheffield had been capable of an act of extraordinary violence and cruelty, the kind more commonly associated with people who came from backgrounds of such extreme deprivation that it inured them to such behavior. Sheffield had no such excuse. He'd come from the heights of privilege—money, power, security—he'd had it all. And he'd used it as a license to indulge the most sordid of instincts.

Why?

Flynn shook his head, throwing water in all directions. He had a tendency to overanalyze situations, and he was probably doing that now but he couldn't get past the feeling that Sheffield's behavior was so extreme there had to be some clear-cut explanation for it.

What was it Chrissie had said? "Everyone knew to give Lewis a wide berth." She'd been talking about the town kids like herself, but how would they have known? At the time of the attack, Lewis had been at the school a year, not an inconsiderable length of time but also not long enough to have had much of an impact on the people outside of Hawkins. What had he done that had brought him to everyone's attention so quickly?

Cursing himself for not picking up on that immediately, he got out of the shower. With a towel tied around his hips and water still dripping from his hair, he left the bedroom and went into the kitchen. The LeMoix's number was listed in the local directory. He punched it in and waited.

Patrick answered on the fourth ring. He sounded tired but alert, like a man who wants to rest but can't. "Yeah?"

"It's Corbett. I'm sorry to bother you but there's something Chrissie said that I need to clear up. Is she awake?"

"No, she's not. Listen, I really hate to wake her. She needs to rest. Can this wait?"

"If it has to, but maybe you can help. She said the town kids knew to stay away from Lewis, they knew he was trouble. How did they know? I mean, unless I'm wrong, in situations like this there usually isn't that much mixing between the locals and the preppies, is there?"

"Not usually," Patrick agreed. "People tend to keep their distance. But I seem to remember her telling me that he'd been involved in other things, some vandalism, stealing, stuff like that. The school put up with it because of his family, but the word got around town that he was no good."

"Does that kind of thing happen often?" Flynn asked.

"Not really. Basically the Hawkins kids behave themselves. But every once in a while there's an exception. Sheffield was about the worst."

"His brother went to the school before him. Did you know that?"

"No," Patrick said, "can't say that I did. What's that got to do with it?"

"Maybe nothing, but I'm starting to get a picture in my mind. The brother was Mr. Perfect, right on target on everything. Lewis, on the other hand, comes across as a totally different story. It's almost as though he wanted to put as much distance between himself and his brother as he possibly could."

"If you say so. It doesn't excuse what he did."

"Of course not. I'm not trying to excuse it. I just want to understand why he behaved the way he did, why he seemed to feel like he had to lash out at everything and everybody."

"Not everybody," Patrick corrected. "He didn't go around picking on guys his own size. Chrissie was a girl, younger, and nowhere near as strong. She was also scared to death. He made sure he got hold of somebody a whole lot more vulnerable than himself and then he took full advantage of it."

"Yeah," Flynn said slowly, "that about sizes it up. Listen, thanks for your help."

"Sure. You need anything else, you let me know."

They hung up a few moments later. Flynn sat on the counter stool, his mind racing. The movie studio, Lewis's movies, the violence in them. Charles at the charity ball, standing cool and collected but with that hint of violence around the edges. Elizabeth, serene and beautiful, eyes like steel. Sheffield's movies hadn't made any money. He couldn't touch the principal in his trust funds. His distributor had let him down. He couldn't pay his people. He stood to lose everything he'd built unless something changed fast.

He thought about that for a while, his eyes growing grim. Finally he stood up and went back to the bedroom. He let the towel drop to the floor, briefly considered putting on a pair of pajamas and decided against it. Instead, he slipped into bed next to Constance. In sleep her body was completely relaxed. He smelled the fragrance of her hair and felt the warmth of her skin as he drew her to him. Holding her protectively in the curve of his body, he slept.

Chapter 15

Constance awoke to the sensation of lips brushing over her breasts. She sighed with pleasure and stretched lazily. Eyes still closed, she moved closer to the source of the caress.

Flynn chuckled softly. In the dim light before dawn he gazed at her body appreciatively. Flushed with sleep, warm and pliant, she was more beautiful than any memory could contain. Slowly, wanting to ease the transition to wakefulness as much as possible, he moved over her. His mouth drifted from her breasts, along the slender line of her throat and back again. He reached a hand gently between her legs, stroking the pink, moist flesh and was rewarded with a soft moan.

Sweet ravishment, he thought, and felt a twinge of guilt. Any comparison to what Sheffield had done and what he was doing now was absurd, of course. But still, she wasn't awake, and while her unconscious was thoroughly consenting it didn't seem quite—

"Flynn?" Constance murmured.

"Yes?"

"Anyone ever tell you that you think too much?"

"You're supposed to be asleep."

"At the risk of adding to your overwhelming confidence, no one could sleep through what you were doing."

"Oh, is that so?" He couldn't help looking pleased with himself.

"Hmm, but you know what they say?"

"No, what's that?"

"Turn about is fair play."

"Hey, wait a minute, I—"

"Shh, this won't hurt a bit. Just close your eyes and think of England."

"You said I think too much . . . of . . ."

A long, passion-drenched time later, when his brain started working again, he remembered he had to call Morgenstern.

"I'll be back," he said, rising from the bed.

"Show off," Constance murmured.

He laughed softly, patted the curve of her derriere and left the room.

Morgenstern was out running, his wife informed Flynn. He was expected back shortly but then had to shower, shave and dress for a breakfast being given by the Urban Police Association. After that he was scheduled to take the kids to the zoo and have lunch with his in-laws, followed by an appearance at a political fund-raiser in the evening.

"Sounds like a full day," Flynn said. "Tell him I can lighten his calendar for the next week or so. All he has to do is give me a call."

"Oh, really?" Cecilia Morgenstern asked. She obviously liked the idea of that. "I'll make sure he gets in touch."

The redoubtable Cecilia was true to her word. Within fifteen minutes the phone rang.

"Thanks for calling in," Ben said. "Saves me the trouble of putting out a missing persons report. You *do* have your lovely client in hand, don't you? She went missing from the hotel, throwing my men, and not incidentally half a dozen hotshot TV reporters, into a panic. I'd have been ready to wring your neck if somebody hadn't spotted that car of yours. You do remember my telling you she shouldn't go anywhere?"

"Come on, Ben, coming up here with me doesn't count. You knew exactly where she was."

"Yeah, I got a fair idea. You're really playing this one differently, aren't you, pal?"

"Trouble is I don't think I'm playing at all," Flynn said.

There was silence for a moment as Ben cogitated on that. He whistled softly. "Had to happen eventually, I just wish your timing was better. The Sheffields are going nuts. Seemed you paid a little visit to Lewis's old school, and they don't like it one bit. Let's see if I can remember everything good old Chuckie dredged up: harassment, unethical behavior, invasion of privacy—"

"Is he adding this to the list he started after the Yohuban thing or is this a new list?"

"Beats me. Anyway, what's up?"

Flynn took a deep breath and swung. "The name Christine LeMoix mean anything to you?"

"Nope, should it?"

"Not really, but you can bet it means plenty to the Sheffields. Twenty years ago they paid her a bundle to keep quiet about being raped by their darling boy."

Ben sucked in his breath sharply. "You sure about this? I mean, Lewis couldn't have been more than a kid himself. He was already batting in that league?"

"All the way. I make it assault, unlawful imprisonment, endangering the welfare of a minor and rape, not to mention his family's dip into bribery and blackmail to hush it all up. It's not a pretty story."

"Holy—listen, who is this girl?"

"She's a woman now, but she was thirteen back then. She lives in the town where the Hawkins School is located. Lewis went there for a year before leaving under 'unspecified' circumstances. I did drop by to see the headmaster yesterday, but he wasn't giving up anything. Christine LeMoix happened to recognize Constance from the TV. She'd been thinking about coming forward, and I guess having us suddenly show up gave her the push she needed. The rest is like I told you."

"Any record of this? I mean, was he actually arrested?"

"No way. I told you, the family paid her to keep quiet."

"So it's her word against his, or actually against theirs since he's dead?"

Flynn sighed. He'd known Morgenstern would react this way but he was hoping it wouldn't happen so fast. "Look," he said, "I'm not trying to get an indictment against him for rape after the fact. What I'm saying is that there's now evidence—concrete evidence—that his behavior with Constance wasn't a first-time thing. He attacked a woman at least once before."

"Twenty years ago with no charge, no testimony, no conviction. Come on, Flynn. I don't know who this Chrissie LeMoix is or where she's coming from. She could have any kind of motive for saying this. Maybe she hates rich people. Maybe she's just crazy. Who knows?"

"You'd know if you'd spoken to her," Flynn said, holding on to his temper by sheer dint of willpower. "And you can. She's afraid of publicity but she's willing to talk with you."

"Nice of her. I'll think about it, but you've got to realize that it's all really coming apart over here. The mayor's on the warpath, and I had the head of the city council on the phone yesterday threatening to have me doing legal briefs in Bangladesh unless I go to the grand jury with this one. Geez, Flynn, what do you expect me to do?"

"What's right, Ben. Damn it, that's what I expect! You can't just dismiss what Chrissie LeMoix's saying and you know it. There's a pattern. Sheffield was a sick man. When he felt scared and inadequate, he had to lash out at people. He picked women and he liked to hurt them."

"What are you now, some kind of armchair psychologist?"

"Every lawyer has to understand what makes people tick, you know that. Lewis was sent away to the school his brother, the superstar, went to. He had to feel like he couldn't hack it. Twenty years later the business he'd built—the only thing that was really his own—was going down the tubes and his family was pressuring him to marry for their convenience. It was the same kind of thing, the stress, the feeling that he wasn't good enough."

"What about in between?" Ben demanded. "We're talking twenty years here. If he was so screwed up, how come he went so long in between slips?"

"I'm not saying he did. With the cover-up the family's pulled before, there could have been a dozen incidents and we wouldn't know it. We just got lucky on this one, that's all."

"I don't know . . . I've always stood by the idea that if you can't take it into court, it doesn't count. What you're telling me would be totally inadmissible. Besides, all this stuff about him feeling inadequate and so on, hell, who doesn't? Nobody goes around hurting women just because of something like that." He was silent for a moment before he said decisively, "You've got to give me something more, Flynn. Or better yet, give it to the family. Get them off my back and you and me got no more problem. *Capisce?*"

"What *capisce?* Ben, neither of us is Italian."

"We're both streetwise, Flynn, or at least you used to be. This thing you and the lady have going is all very nice, but try not to lose touch entirely with reality. Okay?"

Good advice, Flynn thought grudgingly, though it would be a cold day in hell before he'd ever tell Ben that. He hung up the phone without bothering with any of the usual closing pleasantries and stalked back into the bedroom. Constance was still asleep. She lay stretched out on her stomach, her hair spread over the pillow and her face turned slightly to one side. He bent down close to her and studied the petal-soft curve of her mouth, the dark dusting of lashes against her cheeks and the smattering of freckles across the bridge of her nose.

She looked adorable. He wanted nothing so much as to strip off his clothes and climb back into bed with her. Only the knowledge that he was rapidly running out of time stopped him. Briefly he considered waking her to tell her where he was going but he decided against it. She deserved to rest after everything she'd been through.

Back in the kitchen he scrawled a quick note and stuck it on the refrigerator. He slung a jacket over his shoulder and checked to make sure he had his keys. It was just after 9:00 a.m. when he let himself out.

Fifteen minutes later the phone rang. Constance turned over groggily. The sound wrenched her from a deep well of sleep.

"Flynn..." she murmured, her hand groping across the bed.

Nothing, only a faint residue of warmth echoing where his body had lain.

The phone continued to ring. Reluctantly she got out of bed. The morning air was cool. She shivered and reached for a blanket to wrap around herself.

In the kitchen she half noticed the absence of any sign of Flynn, no coffee going, no hint of breakfast, no shower running, before she picked up the receiver.

"Hello."

A man's voice, deep and cultured, holding a hint of surprise and something else she couldn't identify, at least not right away, spoke. "Is Mr. Corbett there?"

"No, I don't think so. I'm sorry, he seems to have gone out." Her eyes fell on the refrigerator door where a note was attached. She leaned forward, reading it. Half to herself she said, "He's gone to New York." Why? What on earth could have taken him there so abruptly without even bothering to wake her?

As she pondered the question, the man on the other end of the phone said, "I said . . . what a shame. Perhaps you could give him a message for me?"

"Certainly."

"This is Charles Sheffield. Please tell him my mother would like him to know how very much she appreciated his visit. She's been feeling much better since she realized everything really is in good hands."

Constance's mouth went dry. She stood, wrapped in the blanket, her hand gripping the telephone receiver until the knuckles shone white. "Would you say that again, please?"

"Certainly. My name is Charles Sheffield. I would like Mr. Corbett to know how very pleased my mother was to meet with him. And, I might add, how very pleased I am myself. It's a great relief to us all. You will tell him that, won't you?"

"Yes," Constance said. Her voice seemed to be coming from a great distance. "Yes, I'll certainly tell him."

"Good. Thanks very much. Sorry to have disturbed you."

She set the phone down, her eyes focused on it unseeingly. After a time, she wasn't sure how long, she became aware of how very cold she felt. She went back into the bedroom and methodically set about the business of dressing, not stopping until she was finished. Then she went into the living room and sat down. She stared straight ahead at the empty fireplace. Her thoughts were in turmoil. Charles Sheffield calling Flynn. To thank him for meeting with Elizabeth Sheffield. To say how glad they were everything was working out.

Flynn had betrayed her. For money, for political advantage, it didn't matter. Nothing mattered, save for the fact that no other conclusion was possible. Yet everything in her screamed out against it. She couldn't believe that the man who had made love to her with such tender intensity could have been nothing more than a user and a manipulator. It simply didn't add up.

"Come on," she murmured to herself, "think. The phone rang and I answered it, Sheffield asked for Flynn, I saw the note, told him he was in New York and then he said what he said." She stopped for a moment, a suspicion dawning. "What if he recognized my voice or if he just knew I was up here? He could have seen an opportunity to cause trouble and taken it."

The habit of talking to herself wasn't a new one; it usually came upon her in times of stress. She didn't mind. It helped to speak her thoughts out loud, especially when they were so contradictory and difficult to grasp.

Was Flynn a user and betrayer? Or was Charles Sheffield a particularly clever liar? She knew which one she wanted to believe. But still she hesitated. She had given so much of herself to Flynn, trusted him so much, that she had to know whether or not she had been right to do so.

She hesitated only a moment before going back into the kitchen and picking up the phone. She called information in New York, put the phone down and dialed again.

"Hello," a woman said.

"Mrs. McWhirter, it's Constance. I'm sorry to bother you at home on a Sunday but I need to get in touch with Flynn. Have you heard from him?"

"Why, no. He left a note for me that he was going up to the cabin with you. You are there, aren't you?"

"Oh, yes, and everything's fine. It's just that he left me a note that he had to go into New York, and I thought he might have called you."

"No, I haven't heard from him at all but if I do, I'll let him know you want to talk with him."

"Thanks. Oh, just one other thing. Do you think he might have gone over to see Elizabeth Sheffield again? I could call him there."

It was a risky try and Constance knew it. She managed to sound as casual as she possibly could but her heart was beating wildly.

Helen hesitated before she replied. "Uh . . . I don't know. It's possible. Do you want her number?"

"On second thought, I'll just wait to hear from him. Thanks, though."

She put the phone down but this time she didn't stay where she was. Instead, she made a beeline for the bathroom, where she hung over the sink thinking that she was going to be sick. It didn't happen but it was a close call and when it was over, she was trembling. Tears burned her eyes. She wanted desperately to cry, messy though it would be, but she couldn't manage it. All the anger and fear caused by Flynn's betrayal remained bottled up inside her, exactly where it could do the most possible damage.

Her clearest instinct was to flee, but how and to where? He'd taken the Checker and she had no transportation. And even if she had, she couldn't go back to the city with the media still on a rampage, yet neither could she run any farther without bringing down the wrath of the D.A. Like it or not, she was well and truly trapped. Flynn had seen to that.

No, correction. She had seen to it herself. By falling in love with him and casting anything resembling caution to the four winds.

Damn him.

All right, that was the way it was and she was going to have to deal with it. But how? The thought of having to wait however many hours until he returned was more than she could bear.

She glanced around the beautiful, cheerful room and was struck again by the incongruity of what was happening. How could a man who could patiently and skillfully create so much be capable of such destructiveness?

Wearily she shook her head. She wasn't going to find any answers, only variations on the same questions. There was nothing for her within the four walls of the cabin. And she needed to move, to at least have the illusion of action. She got up, took a sweater from the closet without looking at it and went out, letting the door bang shut behind her.

Chapter 16

Flynn shook his head in disgust. Nothing was going his way. First he'd run smack into a major-league traffic jam heading sound toward the city. By the time he'd finally worked his way around that and hit Manhattan, it was midafternoon. Rather than waste time going to his apartment he pulled over at the first pay phone he saw and took out the little black book he never failed to carry.

He riffled through the pages, noting as he did that in his case the term "little black book" definitely gave the wrong impression. Anyone seeking clues to his social life would have been disappointed. The numbers there were strictly business. Two had been added recently under the S's. Elizabeth Sheffield, and right below it, Charles Sheffield. Not strictly alphabetical, but an accurate reflection of where they stood in relation to each other.

He dialed Charles's number, waited while it was answered and then gave his name.

"I am sorry, sir," a very proper British voice intoned, "but Mr. Sheffield is not in at the moment. May he return the call?"

"When do you expect him back?"

"I really cahn't say, sir. Is there a message?"

There was but it didn't bear repeating. Flynn got off the phone but stayed in the booth. He'd be damned if he'd tear himself away from Constance for nothing. He thought for a moment and reached for the phone again.

Unlike Sheffield, Delia Russell was at home. She was surprised to hear from him, and he half expected her to hang up. Instead, she threw him one of those long, slow curves that can make the business of lawyering so interesting.

"I suppose it would be all right," she said in a soft voice underlaid with a hint of steel magnolia. "I do have a date this evening, but you did say you wouldn't need much time."

"That's right," Flynn said, his mind busily turning over her statement. Sheffield wasn't even buried yet—that was scheduled for the next day—and the woman he was rumored to have been planning to marry had a date. Whoever said love was fleeting didn't know the half of it.

"I'll be there in ten minutes," he assured her. In fact, he made it in five.

Delia Russell lived in a cooperative at Dutton Place. For those who cared about such things, that spoke volumes. During the rah-rah days of the 1980s, the co-op apartment market in Manhattan went nuts. It seemed as if everybody and his grandmother wanted to buy one. Prices went through the ceiling, which oddly enough had the effect of loosening previously ironclad restrictions on who got to be a co-op owner and who didn't. Time was you didn't, unless you met the co-op board's idea of who was desirable. A few buildings let in actors, for instance, but most didn't. And members of minorities could forget the whole thing right from the start.

But come the Eighties and it was open season, a pure democracy of the pocketbook—with certain exceptions. Dutton Place was one of them. Even as prices for apartments there went well into the seven figures, the same old restrictions held. You didn't get in unless you were old line, old money and old boy.

Or, as in Delia's case, your daddy was.

Delia herself was in her early twenties, five feet something and petite but curvy, with shoulder-length blond hair and big, heavily lashed blue eyes. She greeted Flynn wearing classic tailored trousers, a silk blouse buttoned up to the collar and a smile that said look but don't touch.

The apartment was pure nouveau Victorian—fluttery lace curtains, lots of indecipherable pictures in gilt frames, chintz fabrics, floral rugs, even a ceramic pug dog gazing soulfully from its perch beside the fireplace.

"Sit down," Delia said, gesturing to the settee that was so heaped with needlepoint pillows—done by herself?—that there was virtually no room left to do so. Flynn solved that problem by simply pushing a bunch of them into one corner. He ignored his hostess's frown and got down to business.

"As I told you on the phone, I represent Constance Lehane." Ethics required him to be real straight on that, and he had no problem with it. Instinct told him the straighter he was with Miss Delia I-do-have-a-date Russell, the better.

"Miss Lehane is being investigated in the matter of Lewis Sheffield's death. It is our position that the investigation is without merit. I'd like to talk with you about Lewis, get some insights into his character, to try to understand what happened between them."

"I see...." she said slowly. She settled herself more comfortably in the wing chair across from him and reached for a small marble box on the adjacent table. From it she withdrew a cigarette, which she held extended between two slender fingers, waiting.

It took Flynn a moment to get the idea. He couldn't remember the last time he'd lit a cigarette for a woman but he did so now, using a pack of matches he found crumpled in his pocket along with the other standard but rarely used equipment he carried with him, like the cigarettes, a length of string he couldn't imagine ever using but kept nonetheless and a Swiss Army knife with which he had once broken out of a food locker where an irate member of organized crime had deposited him after Flynn refused to take his case. Clever folks, those Swiss.

The matches were from Harry's Diner in the Bronx and admittedly had seen better days. The ad on the inside explaining how refrigerator repair could be learned in your spare time was almost worn through. Flynn tossed the matches on the table, shoved a few more of the pillows aside and smiled.

It was the smile prosecutors hated to see because it meant Flynn Corbett was moving in for the kill. Juries, on the other hand, loved it.

"I'm glad you see, Miss Russell," he said. "You're a lot younger than I thought you'd be." That was a lie; he'd known going in exactly how old she was. But ethics only went so far.

She looked at him quizzically, her interest piqued. In Delia Russell's book younger was always better than older, at least for women. But it was possible to have too much of a good thing. *Too* young meant childlike, which wasn't good at all. She frowned again, trying to figure out whether Flynn had complimented her or not.

"What do you mean?" she asked.

"Sheffield was thirty-four years old when he died, which makes you what, thirteen, fourteen years younger than he was?"

In fact, he knew it made her eleven years younger, but a little exaggeration couldn't hurt.

The frown disappeared. She bestowed a smile. "That's hardly an unheard of age difference in couples, is it, Mr. Corbett?"

"I guess not. Anyway, it is true the two of you were going to be married?"

She hesitated again. He sat back, content to watch her. Delia Russell was one of those women he'd managed to avoid, the kind who calculated every move. Just then she was busy trying to decide whether admitting to Sheffield's marital intentions was to her benefit or not. Finally she said, "It had been discussed, but we hadn't made a final decision."

Maybe so, but Flynn was willing to bet Elizabeth Sheffield and Daddy Russell had made up *their* minds, and that was all that really counted. Gently he said, "Lewis's death must have come as a terrible shock to you."

"Oh, yes," she replied. Dutifully she added, "Lewis was a wonderful man. It was a privilege just to know him. I can still hardly believe he's gone."

"A really brilliant filmmaker, too. Right?"

"Oh, yes, that, too."

Not bad, she'd learned the script almost letter-perfect. It was time for a little improvisation.

"How did he get along with his brother?"

Delia drew back slightly. "What?"

"His brother, how did he and Charles get along?"

"F-fine. They got along fine. Now, if there's nothing else, Mr. Corbett—"

"Really? That surprises me. I had the impression they didn't get along well at all." Actually the suspicion was founded on little more than gut instinct, but there was no reason for her to know that.

"You did? I hadn't . . . that is—"

"I mean, Charles was always the one who did everything right, and he was trusted with the family business. Whereas Lewis had a lot of problems along the line, didn't he? And all he had was that studio, which was going belly-up any day now."

"How did you know . . . ?"

Flynn shrugged as though it was the most obvious thing in the world. "What I can't figure out is why Lewis didn't just tell his brother he needed the money. I mean, they were brothers, after all, even if th didn't get along so great. Surely Charles would have helped him out."

"He did ask him—" Delia stopped again, flustered, and stabbed the cigarette out. "I'm not really sure I should be talking with you about this."

"Why?" He grinned again. "Didn't good old Charles cover this part when he briefed you on what to say? Or was it Elizabeth who ran you through your paces? She comes across as one tough old gal, let me tell you. I don't blame you for being afraid to cross her."

Delia's pretty porcelain coloring had faded to a sickly gray. She stared at Flynn in horrified fascination, not unlike the mongoose observing the snake.

"I don't know what you're talking about. You have to leave now."

"If you say so, but I can't figure out what's in it for you. Lewis is dead, there isn't going to be a marriage, and from what I can tell, you should be down on your knees thanking God for that. I mean, the guy was strictly trouble when it came to women."

"I wouldn't know." She stood up, shaking slightly. "You have to go."

Flynn also stood. He towered over her by a good foot, but any hesitation he might have felt about the advantage that gave him was washed out by the thought of Constance. Relentlessly he said, "You wouldn't know? Does that mean you and he never—?"

She shot him a look of extreme displeasure, strode over to the door and yanked it open. "Goodbye, Mr. Corbett."

Flynn followed, but slowly. He looked down at her, his expression almost pitying. "You were going to marry him, Miss Russell. Your father wanted it and Elizabeth Sheffield wanted it—it was a done deal. But Lewis still kept you at arm's length, didn't he? Didn't that strike you as strange?"

For a moment he thought she was going to hit him. She looked overwhelmingly offended, hurt and frightened all at the same time. But Delia Russell wasn't a woman who could sustain anger for very long. She had been schooled to acceptance, to letting other people make the decisions and bear the responsibility. Her part was to look attractive and do as she was told. None of which meant she was stupid, far from it.

Abruptly she seemed to come to a decision. The stiffness left her and she relaxed, as though she'd done everything that could be expected of her and the rest was up to somebody else. Quietly she said, "No, it didn't. Lewis made it clear to me from the beginning that our marriage would not involve any kind of intimacy. He kept that part of his life very private, very separate. I accepted that."

Flynn could have asked why any healthy young woman would agree to such an arrangement but he didn't have to. Delia told him herself. "Once he was married, Lewis would finally have access to the trust funds in his name. In addition, I was due to receive a very large cash settlement from both our families. We would have been free to go our own ways so long as we kept up the formality of being husband and wife. wanted that freedom very much. I still do."

"I don't understand," Flynn admitted. "There's nothing to indicate that Sheffield was either homosexual or impotent. Why would he want such an arrangement?"

"You're Constance Lehane's lawyer—you should be able to figure that out for yourself. But if you can't—" She paused and looked straight at him. "If you can't, ask Charles."

"Ah, yes, Charles. I keep coming back to him."

"So did Lewis. It's an unpleasant story but not a totally unusual one. You won't hear it from me," she added quickly, "but I will say you seem to be on the right track."

"How come you're willing to help that much? After all, you were almost a Sheffield."

She flashed him a sudden smile, giving him a glimpse of the woman she might have been if money and position hadn't counted so overwhelmingly with her. "'Almost' only counts in horseshoes. Besides, the Sheffields have had enough from me."

And that, so far as Delia Russell was concerned, was that. She shut the door softly behind him. He went down the carpeted hallway, pushed the button for the elevator and stood lost in thought waiting for it to appear.

One thing was sure: Lewis's relationship with his brother lay at the heart of the problem. He had to find Charles and he had to do it fast. The problem was where to start. Since no immediate solution presented itself, he decided to call Constance first. He wanted to tell her what he'd learned from Delia; more than that, he simply wanted to hear her voice. But Constance wasn't answering the phone. He let it ring ten times before he gave up and called Helen at home instead.

"Sorry to bother you on a Sunday," he said, "but I figured I'd better check in. Everything okay at the office?"

He expected a routine response regarding the status of his various cases, the disposition of his partners and any useful or amusing gossip that might have cropped up. Instead, he got something altogether different.

"Where are you?" Helen demanded. "Constance called earlier. I've got this terrible feeling I said something wrong."

"What's wrong?" Helen, goof? That was virtually incomprehensible. What could she possibly have said?

"She asked me if you might have gone to see Elizabeth Sheffield *again,* and before I could think, I said maybe you had. Did you tell her about seeing that woman in the first place?"

"No," Flynn said quickly. A sick feeling threatened to envelop him. He should have told her and he'd meant to, but none of that mattered now. All that counted was that he hadn't.

"Then how else could she have found out?" Helen asked.

"I don't know. Did she sound upset?"

"No, she was very cool. *Too* cool, if you know what I mean. As though everything was just fine when it couldn't possibly be. Flynn—" In moments of extreme tension, Helen called him by his first name. "That girl, woman, whatever, has got a lot of substance to her, but she's going through an awfully tough time. And finding out that you'd gone to see Mrs. Sheffield must have her in an awful state."

"I just tried to call her," Flynn said, half to himself. "There was no answer."

"Could she have left the cabin?"

"Not for any real distance. I took the car."

"Then maybe she just went for a walk. Can you wait a bit and call her again?"

"Yeah," he said slowly, "I guess so." That was the logical thing to do but it went against the sense of urgency that was steadily growing within him.

He hated—really hated, with an intensity that shocked him—the way Constance must be feeling right now. The idea of her thinking that he'd betrayed her, that what they'd shared had been false in any way, went through him like a knife. Charles Sheffield would have to wait. He had to see Constance, to speak with her and hold her, to stop the hurt he knew she must be experiencing. Nothing else mattered as much.

"I'm going back to the cabin," he said quickly. "Do me a favor and call Ben Morgenstern's house. Tell him I expect to be meeting with the Sheffields at the earliest opportunity and that the matter will be taken care of. He'll know what that means."

"I'm glad he does," Helen said with a sniff, "since I most certainly don't. This is all highly irregular."

"Just give him the message. If he's got any idea of putting the case on the docket for the grand jury this week, tell him to forget it. He'll just end up with egg on his face."

"All right," Helen said slowly, "I'll tell him for whatever good it'll do. He'll want to talk with you directly."

"I'll be in touch as soon as I can. If Constance calls again, tell her I'm on my way. Tell her not to worry, I can explain everything. Tell her..."

"Yes," Helen said gently.

"Never mind, I'll tell her myself." In absolutely unmistakable terms that would leave her with no shred of doubt about his feelings or his intentions. Then he'd deal with the Sheffields, and once that was done—

But first he had to get back to Connecticut. The sun was slanting westward as he left the city behind. Pink and purple clouds drifted over the horizon. It was a perfect evening, but there was a hint of chill in the air as if a weather front were moving in. Further north in Vermont the forecast was for just that, a cold front that was to be accompanied by a late-spring snow.

Chapter 17

Constance pushed away the plate with the remains of a sandwich that she had only half eaten. She was still hungry, but the thought of putting more food in her stomach held no appeal. Neither did anything else she could think of doing.

She had walked for more than an hour in the morning, exploring the area around the cabin in all directions. In the process she discovered a beautiful, secluded pool where she sat for a while, watching the play of light on the water. Inevitably her thoughts turned to Flynn. Try though she did, she couldn't reconcile what Charles Sheffield had let drop with the man she believed she had come to know. There was an essential contradiction that couldn't be overcome. Either she was totally, hopelessly wrong about Flynn or—

Or what? He had gone to Elizabeth Sheffield's apartment, Helen had confirmed that. If he'd told her about it, discussed it with her, she might have understood. But he hadn't. The same man who was able to remember the date of the founding of the Hawkins School because of a check he'd run on an assistant D.A. twelve years before had let that essential piece of information slip his mind. Or he'd deliberately refrained from telling her for his own reasons.

She got up and took the plate to the sink. She set the remains of the sandwich aside, ran water on the plate and left it to dry. With the leftovers in hand she went back outside and sat down on a rock in the sun. Slowly, thinking as she did so, she tore off bits of the sandwich and tossed them on the ground. Immediately a hungry starling swooped down, followed by a blue jay and several blackbirds. They made short work of her uneaten lunch and continued pecking the ground hopefully.

Constance went back into the house, found the rest of the loaf of bread and took it outside. For half an hour she sat feeding the birds until the bread was gone. Only then did she notice that the weather was changing.

The sun was gone behind a line of graying clouds that hung low in the sky. A brisk wind blew out of the north. She shivered and went back inside. The fireplace looked inviting with logs already laid in it. She struck a match and held it to the kindling, watching as it caught. When the fire was going well, she curled up on the couch. Despite the relatively early hour, it was already growing dark outside. Through the window she could see the rock where she'd been sitting. There was no sign now of the birds.

Flynn had a more than ample collection of books scattered all through the cabin. She picked up a mystery but barely glanced at it. The book remained open but unread in her lap. She stared into the fire, conscious of the sense of waiting for something to happen. Flynn would return, they would talk, and then—

By afternoon it was snowing steadily. Several inches had already covered the ground and more was clearly on the way. Constance switched on the radio and listened to a forecast that promised more than a foot of snow before dawn. Ordinarily that would have cheered her, but she was worried about Flynn getting back. When she heard the crunch of tires on the gravel road she breathed a sigh of relief. Whatever else was going on, at least he was safe.

But when she went to the window and looked out, it wasn't the Checker she saw. Instead, a Range Rover was parked just far enough away that she couldn't make out who was behind the wheel. She waited, thinking perhaps someone had gotten lost and would come to the door to ask for directions. But when several minutes passed without anyone getting out, she began to wonder if perhaps the driver could be ill. After all, why would anyone drive up to a strange house and not leave the car? If whoever was out there was looking at a map, trying to figure out where they were, they would have switched on a light to see by. But the Rover's interior remained dark.

Constance had never been too good about not involving herself in other people's problems. Maybe it was her sturdy midwestern upbringing or simply some essential part of her character, but she always felt compelled to help. She found a pair of men's boots in the closet, Flynn's undoubtedly. They were much too big for her, but she could manage in them. Wrapped in a sheepskin jacket, also his, she trudged outside.

The Rover was parked about ten yards from the house, but the snow was falling thickly enough to make it hard for her to see it clearly. She kept her head down until she had almost reached the car. A man was sitting in the driver's seat; otherwise the vehicle was empty. He had his face turned away from her.

She knocked on the window gently so as not to startle him too much.

"Excuse me, are you all right?"

The man turned. His smile was chilling. There was a light in the cold gray eyes that made her take a quick step back.

He opened the car door swiftly and got out. A hand in a black leather glove grabbed her arm. Still smiling, Charles Sheffield said, "You are remarkably predictable, Miss Lehane. If I'd knocked on the door, you wouldn't have let me in. But this way—"

He gave her a hard push toward the cabin. "Inside. You and I are going to have a little chat."

"We have nothing to talk about," Constance said, struggling to hide the fear growing within her. She tried to pull her arm loose, but he tightened his grip deliberately, hurting her.

"Don't be a fool," Charles said. "I'm going to talk and you're going to listen. This nonsense has gone on long enough."

"You mean the nonsense about your brother getting his kicks hurting women? It seems like he wasn't the only one in the family."

"Why you . . ." He raised his other hand as though to hit her but thought better of it. "Inside," he said harshly.

"Flynn's back," Constance said. "He'll be very angry about this. You won't like—"

"You're a poor liar, Miss Lehane. Mr. Corbett is in New York, you told me that yourself. Given the weather, it's unlikely he'll try to return today, but even if he did, he would be hours behind me." His smile deepened. "We have plenty of time."

"For what?" Constance demanded. She was shaking but told herself it was only from the cold. Lewis Sheffield had frightened her badly; she refused to let his brother do the same. Or at least she tried. There was something about Charles, an icy detachment Lewis had lacked, that made him seem even more threatening.

"We have nothing to say to each other," she insisted as he shoved the door open and all but threw her inside. She stumbled, unable to keep her balance in the oversize boots, and fell.

She moaned softly, caught herself and gritted her teeth. She'd come down hard on her elbow and the pain was significant, but she wouldn't admit that to Charles. Instead, she got up slowly, keeping her eyes on him while she kicked the boots off.

"Go sit down," he ordered, pointing to the living room. She did as he said, conscious with every step of him following her. She took a seat on one of the couches; he remained standing. He looked her over deliberately, his gaze lingering until she felt her skin crawl. Whatever he saw seemed to satisfy him.

"You really are a beautiful woman. I can understand why Lewis wanted you." He spoke matter-of-factly, as though there had been nothing out of the ordinary about Lewis's behavior.

Sickened and provoked by that, Constance snapped, "I suppose you'd say the same about Chrissie Le-Moix."

Charles's eyebrows shot up. She had the satisfaction of knowing she'd hit home before his customary mask slipped back into place.

"So you know about that, do you? Very impressive, but then Mother did warn me that Mr. Corbett wasn't to be underestimated."

"Was that before or after her meeting with him?" Constance asked. She couldn't quite keep the bitterness out of her voice. Sheffield picked up on it at once.

"Both," he said. "Mother has a habit of repeating herself. At any rate, she said he'd be trouble and she was right. We did our best to cover all the bases, but there were bound to be a few we couldn't manage."

"You realize," Constance said boldly, "that if this does go to the grand jury, there's going to be a lot of publicity. In fact, I'll make sure of that by making myself available to every Tom, Dick and Harry reporter who wants an interview. There's a good chance other women will come forward with stories similar to Chrissie's."

Charles shrugged. He stood with his back to the mantel, enjoying the fire. He'd left his jacket near the door and was dressed in gray slacks, a turtleneck pullover and a cardigan. With his hair neatly trimmed and his face gravely handsome, he appeared every inch the proper gentleman.

A wave of revulsion washed over Constance. "You didn't care about your brother at all, did you?"

"On the contrary, we had a rather intense relationship, but that's neither here nor there now. Personally I was very tired of covering for Lewis, always protecting him from the follies of his own actions. If it were left up to me, I'd bury him and be done with it. But Mother feels differently."

"Oh?" Constance said slowly. A plan was beginning to form in her mind. If she could keep Charles talking long enough, it might relax his guard, giving her an opportunity to get away. Still wrapped in Flynn's sheepskin jacket, she leaned back against the couch pillows and managed a faint smile of her own.

"I guess that's the way it goes sometimes with the youngest child. They can do no wrong."

"Unfortunately true. Mother is genuinely convinced that you must be lying. She simply won't have it any other way. Mr. Corbett, on the other hand, seems determined to keep probing into Lewis's background until he uncovers enough dirt to make it clear you're telling the truth."

"So what?" Constance asked. "You just made it clear that you didn't like your brother, so why should you object to your mother finding out what he was really like?"

"Because, dear Miss Lehane, Mother wouldn't be content with that. She would insist on knowing how her darling boy could have become such a bastard. Once she started asking, she wouldn't stop until she got to the bottom of it."

"I see," Constance said slowly. She thought back to what Dominique had said about the Sheffield boys being the product of a marriage that excluded virtually everyone else, of their parents turning them over to servants and boarding schools from the tenderest age.

"Mrs. Sheffield was a lousy mother," she said bluntly, "and maybe that's partly to blame for what Lewis became. But there's more to it than that, isn't there?"

Charles's face flamed. For the first time he showed a reaction stronger than restrained annoyance or cold amusement. "Don't you dare say that about Mother," he said. "She was an angel—beautiful, perfect. I remember her coming in to say good-night when she and Father were on their way to some party. She was the most exquisite thing I'd ever seen. She would laugh and—" He broke off, shaking his head as though to clear it.

"Never mind. The point is that you couldn't possibly comprehend Mother and neither could Lewis. He never appreciated her properly, always whining and complaining about how she wasn't 'there' for him. I had no choice but to punish him for it. He couldn't be allowed to object to her in any way."

Constance took a deep breath, trying to calm the sick feeling in her stomach. It was all too clear now. Lewis had been a violent, resentful man who satisfied his anger by hurting women. But there was an explanation for his behavior, not an excuse but a reason for what had made him the way he was: his brother with his own sick fixation on their mother and his willingness to "punish" the younger brother who didn't share it.

She was reminded of something else Dominique had said, that the children of the very wealthy often led lives that weren't remotely what other people imagined. Constance would have to tell her how right she was, if she got the chance.

"Why are you here?" she asked shakily. "Not just to tell me all this. There has to be another reason."

Charles sighed. The release of his own emotions seemed to have wearied him. He came closer and sat down on the couch near her.

Constance fought the urge to recoil. She remained very still, willing herself to do nothing that would provoke him.

"I want you to call Ben Morgenstern and tell him that you accept full responsibility for Lewis's death. You were angry at him because of his involvement with Delia Russell and you deliberately caused him to fall, striking his head."

"But that's a lie, I did no such thing! If I say that, I'll be confessing to murder."

"Actually to manslaughter. That means you caused his death without premeditation and that you acted without intending him to die. You will express extreme regret and contrition. A lawyer I will provide— not Mr. Corbett—will assist you in plea-bargaining the charge down to death by negligence. Mr. Morgenstern can be expected to go along with this, as it's the most expeditious way of settling the case. Since you have no prior record, you can expect a sentence of probation."

Constance was shaking her head vehemently. "This won't work. In the first place I won't do it. There's no way I'd wreck my life by confessing to something I didn't do. In the second place you can't believe your mother would be satisfied with such an outcome. She'd be furious that someone who admitted to being responsible for her son's death didn't go to jail for it."

He smiled tolerantly. "You don't understand Mother. I'm the only one who ever has. She's not so much concerned with revenge for Lewis's death. After all, it's not as though she cared about him. What she can't bear to admit is that anything she did turned out less than perfectly. Having a son like Lewis would be a terrible blow to her image of herself. Better you should go relatively scot-free than to have questions raised about his behavior."

"What about Delia Russell? Your mother engineered that whole relationship for business reasons, didn't she? Lewis's death frustrated her plans. Will she be so willing to forgive me for that?"

"Tom Russell, Delia's father, is as anxious for a merger as we are. It will take place as planned, merely without the matrimonial trappings. Provided no scandal taints the Sheffield name. Our reputation is sacrosanct, nothing must be allowed to affect that."

Constance privately thought that was a crock. All this emphasis on honor, name and public image was disgusting in light of what had actually been going on. She almost said as much. Only the instinct for self-preservation stopped her.

"All right," she said, "I understand you think you're doing what's best for your own interests, bu that doesn't change the fact that I won't cooperate. I have absolutely no reason to do so."

Charles leaned closer. She felt the heat of his body and was surprised by its intensity. Softly, almost gently, he said, "Oh, but you do, Miss Lehane. Unless you do exactly as I say, you're going to be badly hurt."

"You're crazy!" Discretion be damned—there was only so much she could listen to. "If you do anything to me, everyone will know. Flynn will tear you apart You won't—"

"Mr. Corbett won't be in a position to do anything about it. I am a very wealthy and powerful man, Miss Lehane. I have the resources to get essentially anything I want, and I have given careful thought to how to do so in this particular instance. Mr. Corbett has made no effort to conceal the fact that his relationship with you is personal. You are obviously very involved with one another. Now, either you do as I say or he will suffer. Do I make myself clear?"

Bile burned the back of Constance's throat. Her mind reeled. "You can't...Flynn is too smart for you, too tough . . . you won't be able to . . ."

"Do you really want to take the risk? You shouldn't because I assure you, you'll regret it. Unless, of course, I'm wrong about your feelings for Mr. Corbett. There is that possibility. However, I think, all things considered, that you really do care for him. Believe me, I won't hesitate. You call Mr. Morgenstern now, then you leave here with me and have no further contact with Mr. Corbett. Otherwise, he dies."

"For what?" Constance gasped. This was far worse than anything she had feared. She had a terrible sense of having stepped into a different reality, where none of the rules she understood applied. "You'd kill a man to protect your family's reputation, is that what you're saying?"

"Of course," he replied, surprised that she would find anything unusual in that. "Reputation, the way one is perceived in the world, is the greatest possible asset. Without it one is unacceptably vulnerable. Easy pickings for those who wouldn't hesitate to take advantage. Lewis was a chink in our armor, a weak link. We're well rid of him, but only if his death isn't allowed to become an opening through which others can strike at us."

"You have a warped view of the world," Constance said. "What makes you think anybody really cares about what's going on in your family? People have their own lives to worry about."

"One thing makes me think that, Miss Lehane." His eyes glittered. He took hold of her again, putting pressure on her wrist. "We are very, very rich. Richer than you can imagine. Our wealth opens us to envy and hatred that could destroy us, *if* we show any weakness. I absolutely refuse to do that.

"Now," he added, standing up, "you're going to make that call."

He dragged her over to the kitchen counter and reached for the phone. At the same instant Constance acted. Whatever rarified world Charles Sheffield inhabited—some weird mix of Fifth Avenue apartments, exclusive prep schools and assassins for hire—it hadn't prepared him to deal with a down-home Ohio girl who had her dander up. With Lewis she'd been taken by surprise and hardly able to cope; only chance had saved her. This was different. She'd had enough time to come to terms with exactly what Charles Sheffield was and how to deal with him. To hell with the niceties—in a spot like this she did exactly what her mother had always told her to do.

It worked. Even as she was removing her knee from his groin, Sheffield was collapsing like a deflated balloon. Under other circumstances the look on his face might actually have been comical. He was the picture of a man for whom the world has suddenly turned upside down. All his life he'd been the one to dish out pain and humiliation. Suddenly he was getting a heavy dose of it himself.

Constance didn't hang around, though, to appreciate the effect. She raced for the door and tore it open, dashing outside.

Straight into the snow.

Chapter 18

The cold stunned her. The sheepskin jacket she was still wearing helped, but she had kicked off the boots and was barefoot except for wool socks. Snow crunched under her feet as she ran for the Range Rover. If she could only get there before Sheffield recovered, she'd be all right. She could drive into town, get help and—

If he'd left the keys in the ignition. Heart in her mouth, she jerked open the driver's door and felt for the keys. Nothing. She tried again, bending down to see under the steering wheel. Still nothing. Charles had taken the keys into the house with him. The car that should have been her refuge and her escape was no help at all.

Footsteps sounded behind her. She glanced over her shoulder in time to see Sheffield racing from the house. He was still hobbled, running slightly bent over, but fast for all that.

Constance ran. Through the snow and over the uneven ground, heedless of the frigid air burning her lungs, she ran. Sheffield was close behind her. She could hear the harshness of his breathing and the heavy thud of his feet in the snow. Her own were numb. She couldn't feel them or the ground she ran over. Stumbling over a rock, she almost fell but managed to hold herself upright by sheer panic-stricken determination.

A narrow path led off behind the house. Constance had seen it earlier in the day, but now the snow nearly covered it completely. She followed it to the curve of the small pool she had lingered by. Sheffield had begun to lag. She glanced back over her shoulder and saw his face, gray and strained, with high patches of color framing his cheeks. Encouraged, she strained for the last measure of speed and was rewarded when she heard him falter and stop.

She didn't look back again but kept going until she had skirted the edge of the pool and reached the other side. There she finally paused to catch her breath. Through the deep shadows of the trees and the flickering veil of falling snow she could see Sheffield heading back toward the cabin. He was giving up!

Relief filled her until she recognized the path she was on. Beyond lay tractless forest she had no hope of transversing in her present state. The only direction she could go in was back toward the cabin. Sheffield would be there waiting. And she had scant hope of slipping past him while daylight still held.

She glanced at her watch and saw that darkness wouldn't set in for another three hours. Perhaps a little less, given the storm, but even with luck she had a long wait. Abruptly her knees buckled. She fell into the snow and sat for a moment, staring straight ahead. Flecks of white dusted her eyelashes and chilled her lips. Glancing down she realized that she could not feel her feet at all.

For a moment panic filled her. Hard on its heels came the common sense that had always been her saving grace. She had a problem; there was no denying that. But if she let fear get the better of her, she really would be in trouble.

The first thing she had to do was find shelter. That proved easier than she expected. Near the pool was a rock outcropping, the sheer face of which angled inward to create a protected recess. The ground immediately within it was free of snow.

Constance scrambled toward it. Without sensation in her feet, she fell several more times but eventually she made it. Huddled as tightly against the rock as she could manage, she tucked her feet underneath her and pulled the sheepskin jacket down as far as it would go. With the collar turned up and her shoulders hunched, she could no longer feel the snow.

She glanced at the luminous dial of her watch. Three hours at the most. She could survive that. Confidence filled her. The worst was over.

Or so she thought. In fact, it had just begun. Within half an hour of finding the rock outcropping, feeling began to return to her feet. It came in the form of knifelike shards of pain that brought tears to her eyes and made her gasp in agony. Gritting her teeth she told herself the pain meant she was still alive. Taken in that light she should be grateful for it.

That far she could not go, but in another thirty minutes or so the worst of the pain had passed, or perhaps she simply got used to it. At any rate, her discomfort became bearable and she was able to begin thinking about what she would do once she got past the house.

It would be very dark. The cloud cover would prevent any moonlight from showing. She had driven the dirt road with Flynn only twice but she believed she would be able to follow it well enough. Once she got to the main road, she would have to take her chances hitchhiking, presuming, of course, that any vehicles were out on such a night.

Despite everything she smiled. The snowstorm that was giving her such trouble was routine for this part of Connecticut. Not at this time of the year, but during the winter such snowfalls were commonplace. With any luck, people wouldn't hesitate to be out and about.

With any luck. That was all she needed; a little good fortune and she'd be home free. Once she got a ride, she'd make it to town, go to the sheriff's office and tell them what had happened....

They wouldn't believe her. Or they would at the very least be extremely skeptical.

So what? It wasn't critical that they believe her, only that she had sufficient protection until Flynn returned. He would know how to deal with Sheffield. She had absolute faith in him. Flynn would take care of everything. He would—

The wind rippled against her cheek, intruding into the stillness of her shelter. She looked up. Beyond, near the edge of the pond, the tops of the trees had begun to bend. The snow was falling more heavily. It rippled in whirling eddies across the frozen water. Again the wind struck her. She shivered, feeling the cold to her bones. Her feet ached dully, and she had to swallow hard against the moan that threatened to burst from her.

The storm had changed direction. It was blowing straight into the outcropping. Already snow was piling up all around her. What had been her sanctuary had quickly become a trap.

She forced herself to extend a hand beyond the warmth of the jacket, clutching the rock face. Pulling herself up, she gasped as pain shot through her again, all the way up her legs and into the base of her spine. A soft scream broke from her as she collapsed onto the ground.

Long moments passed before she was able to raise her head. Snow struck her full in the face. The wind tore at the rock. She tried to breathe and found the frigid air scalding.

Desperation filled her. She tried again to stand, concentrating every ounce of her strength, and did manage to stand upright. Only to collapse again the moment she let go of the outcropping and placed any weight on her feet.

Lying facedown in the snow, feeling the coldness along every inch of her body, Constance was finally forced to confront an irrefutable conclusion: she could not move. She was trapped, exposed, in the middle of a blizzard.

Beyond that lay another equally inescapable fact. It came surging up out of the darkness of her consciousness, the stuff of distant, unformed futures made suddenly immediate.

She was going to die.

Flynn pulled off the road about an hour south of the cabin. The storm was more intense than he had expected. Although the Checker was equipped with the best all-weather tires, he was still finding it heavy going. Many of the other cars seemed to be equipped with nothing at all. They were slipping and sliding all over the place.

After parking at a rest stop, he went inside, got himself a cup of coffee and stood sipping it, looking out the plate-glass windows at the swirling storm. He wanted to talk to Constance face-to-face, to explain to her, however belatedly, why he had met with Elizabeth Sheffield. But the storm was holding him up, and he had an ill-defined but still powerful sense of precious time passing.

He finished the coffee, tossed the plastic container in a trash can and found a pay phone. By the fourth ring he was frowning. Where was she? She couldn't have left the cabin, and with the weather the way it was, surely she wouldn't be outside.

The shower, maybe? He hung up and went back to the window, forcing himself to wait five minutes before returning for another try. This time he let the phone ring eight times before deciding Constance wasn't going to answer.

He was almost right. When the receiver was picked up, a man's voice said, "Yes?"

Flynn didn't reply. He held the phone an inch or so from his ear and listened to the sound coming from the other end. Static and breathing, very definitely a presence. He hadn't imagined that cautious query.

"Who's this?" he demanded.

Silence again for a moment and then the unmistakable click of the phone being hung up.

Flynn left the rest stop. He got back into the Checker and back onto the highway. It was still snowing heavily. Most cars had slowed to several miles below the speed limit. Flynn ignored them. He was an expert driver in a solid car and he knew his capability. Never mind that he probably scared a good five years off some of the people he passed.

Forty-five minutes later, a full quarter of an hour sooner than he would have made it in average weather, he barreled down the exit ramp and picked up the town road. There the going was easier. The local snowplows had already been out along with the sanders. His own road was a different story. In the winter a neighbor plowed it for him, but the neighbor had gone south on a fishing trip and the road was impassable. Not that he didn't try.

After fishtailing once and almost slamming into a tree, he gave up and abandoned the car. He started out down the road at a brisk walk but before more than a minute or two he was running. He couldn't say why, exactly, only that in the gathering gloom of late afternoon accentuated by the storm he felt an undeniable presence of danger. Experience had taught him not to question his instincts. As he neared the cabin, he slowed down.

He saw the Range Rover as soon as he came around the last bend. Painted white, it almost blended into the surrounding snow but the darker bumper and framing around the windshield made it visible. Flynn paused. He moved back behind a tree and stood staring at the vehicle.

Who did he know who drove a Range Rover? The British import was popular enough in some of the wealthier suburbs around New York, but you didn't see too many of them in this part of Connecticut. This one was parked facing him so he couldn't make out the license, but offhand he couldn't think of any of his neighbors who might be driving it.

His eyes narrowed slightly as he noted that there were no tread marks around the car. For that matter, there were none on the road, either. Whoever owned the Rover must have arrived at the cabin several hours before.

The LeMoixes maybe? He'd left his local address and phone number with them. Could Chrissie and her husband have decided that they needed to talk to him again and finding him absent stayed to chat with Constance? Sure, provided they had roughly thirty thousand dollars to sink into a car and had chosen an import to boot.

Okay, if not the LeMoixes, then who? Some friend of Constance's she'd called to keep her company when she realized he was gone? Not likely, since she'd told him there was no one in the area she really felt comfortable turning to other than Dominique, who had never driven anything with four-wheel drive in her life, believing as she did that automobiles were meant to be long, black and chauffeured.

Flynn's expression hardened. The more he thought about this the less he liked it. The feeling of urgency was still in him and growing stronger by the moment. Something felt very wrong.

He moved forward cautiously toward the cabin, keeping in the shadows as much as he could. A sudden movement at one of the front windows made him drop to his knees out of sight. He looked up, straight through the glass panes he'd set in place himself. On the other side of them, at the far end of the room, he could see the fire going. The cabin looked warm and cheerful as usual except for one element: the face at the window was Charles Sheffield's.

Flynn cursed under his breath. Score one for the butler. Mr. Sheffield was indeed out, *way* out of line. His first impulse was to march in, demand what the hell was going on and scare the daylights out of the creep. But on second thought, he wondered if he shouldn't wait a few minutes and get a better handle on what was actually happening. After all, he hadn't seen Constance yet. She might have everything under control; she might even be gaining some valuable information. He could blow it by barging in.

In law, strategy and timing were everything. Nobody knew that better than Flynn. But it wasn't the lawyer who was standing outside the cabin with nothing on his mind except cracking a case. It was the man, and what he saw didn't satisfy him one little bit.

Where was Constance? Why couldn't he see her? Every suspicion he'd had about Sheffield, especially those that had been verified by Delia Russell, surged to the fore. To hell with the case. He wasn't leaving Constance with him one moment longer.

The front door of the cabin was made of a solid piece of oak braced by old-fashioned iron cross-pieces. It was as solid as they come but it yielded almost at once to the firm pressure of Flynn's shoulder applied to it at high speed and with great sincerity.

It hurt but he hardly noticed. Far more important, and satisfying, was the look of shock on Sheffield's face that gave way quickly to fear.

"W-what . . . ?" the financier said.

Flynn barely slowed his pace. He came across the room swiftly, radiating anger, and took hold of Sheffield, half lifting him off the ground.

"Where is she?" he demanded.

The other man's face was white. He gasped, arms flailing, as the indignity and vulnerability of his position struck him full force.

"You can't do this!" he exclaimed.

Flynn didn't bother to reply, at least not directly. He emphasized the irrelevance of that statement by lifting Charles a few inches higher and pressing him into the nearest wall.

"I'm gonna ask you one more time. Where is she?"

The street tone was deliberate. It was pure hard-nosed Hoboken down by the railroad tracks with the broken glass and the burned-out bums. Rough-and-tough Hoboken, running the rails, daring the 5:14 out of New York to catch you and feeling as though you'd live forever when it didn't.

Not exactly something Charles Sheffield could relate to personally. His struggles had been carried on at a safe distance or against those a whole lot smaller and less assertive than himself, his younger brother, for example.

"Who?" Sheffield croaked.

As questions went, it won no points for brilliance. If he was playing for time, he lost. Flynn took a deep breath and set him down. Sheffield swallowed his surprise, fumbling to smooth his clothes.

"Well, now, that's better. You've really got a nerve—"

"I'm going to hurt you very badly," Flynn said almost casually.

"What are you—?"

"That's why I put you down. Even a piece of excrement like yourself should have a chance to defend himself." The words were tough; the tone they were uttered in was worse. Flynn spoke calmly, even pleasantly. Meanwhile, he took off his jacket and laid it aside. His mother hadn't raised him to be careless with expensive clothes.

Sheffield hesitated a split second but not even he was that dumb. He took one look at the red glint in Flynn's eyes and the white line around his mouth, and decided he was serious.

"I don't know where she is," he blurted. "She wasn't here when I arrived. I was going to leave, but the snow got worse and I was trapped."

He'd come up with that story while he was waiting just in case he happened to need it. That was all part of planning for every contingency, something he prided himself on as his great strength and what a gorilla like Flynn Corbett would never understand.

It might have worked except the *gorilla* had spent the better part of his adult life in a courtroom figuring out who was lying and who wasn't. That was *his* great strength and something the likes of Charles Sheffield couldn't even begin to understand.

"How'd you get in?" Flynn demanded. He raised his fist as he did so and took a quick, hard swipe at Sheffield's chin. The blow was meant only to graze him, a little sample of things to come, but it might as well have been a direct hit considering the reaction it got.

Sheffield jerked his head back and raised his hands, also fisted. He tried to return the blow, but Flynn ducked it easily.

"How about that, Chuckie?" he drawled. "How'd you get in? The door was locked when I left, Constance would have the sense to leave it the same way." Another blow, harder this time. "So what'd you do, climb in a window?" Duck—the guy really couldn't hit the side of a barn. "That's breaking and entering, you know. You could get five to seven for that." One more, letting him really feel it this time all the way up around the eye sockets where the pain gets very unpleasant.

"Talk to me, Chuckie. I got a real bad feeling about this and I'm liable to really start taking it out on you any minute now. Where is she?"

"She ran out," Sheffield blurted. He put his hands up to protect his face and backed into the wall himself. "I didn't do anything to her, I swear. I'm not my brother."

"No, you're worse," Flynn said, unable to hide his disgust. "How long ago?"

"A few hours, that's all. She—"

A few hours. Disbelief roared through him, fol-
ved hard by the inescapable realization that the ur-

gency he had felt earlier had been more than justified. In the cold and the snow...where could she be? Where would she have found shelter?

He took a step toward Sheffield. The gun he habitually carried was a cold weight against the side of his chest. Stamped on his face was the clear intention to have revenge. The other man flinched. He looked sick with terror.

That wasn't what stopped Flynn. He was happy enough to have Sheffield writhing in panic. What made him draw back was the knowledge that time was running out. Indeed, might already be gone.

No, he couldn't think that. He had to find her all right, alive, safe. He had to. Sheffield didn't matter. Constance was everything.

Running out of the cabin, he barely registered the door banging behind him, the coldness hitting him like a wave. Plunging through it and through the shadows, snow crackled beneath his feet, slowing him down.

"Constance!"

His shout bounced off the high maples and the evergreens that framed the cabin. It bounced against the whiteness gleaming beneath the darkening sky. It rang in his own ears, all his desperation there for anyone to hear.

"Constance!"

Nothing. Not even the slightest murmur of a reply. Even the wind was still.

Where could she have gone? Which way of all th ways? To the road? Yes, maybe. No...wait. She field's Range Rover. She would have headed for it.

He ran to the vehicle and looked inside, noticed that the keys were missing and forced himself to stand, absolutely still, scanning the silence. The car, the cabin, Constance running, Sheffield coming after her. Flynn turned, calculating possible directions, thinking...

She would have had one thought only, to get away. He turned again, head high, every sense alert.

The pool. His favorite place, the summer sanctuary of cool water and golden sun. In winter a place to contemplate the stillness. And now, in the interrupted spring, a place for... what? Hiding?

He could be wrong. She might have gone in an entirely different direction. Yet she couldn't have plunged into the forests, and the only other alternative was the road. If she had headed that way, she'd have reached town by now. If she hadn't...

He started running again, flat out, sprinting. The air burned his lungs. Which was fine, because it let him know he was alive. Please God, Constance would be, too.

He skirted the shore, searching. Once a shadow near a pine tree caught his eye, but it was nothing more than an elder bush covered with snow. He moved on. Rabbit tracks crossed his way. Another creature caught out in the storm but one better able to find shelter than Constance.

Where...?

Somewhere beneath the laden clouds the sun was going down in glory, but Flynn couldn't see it. He knew only that the darkness was spreading, growing intensity. Already he was having trouble seeing.

But he could still hear. At first he thought the faint moan was the returning wind. When it came again, he knew a surge of relief so intense as to be agonizing.

Following the sound to the rock outcropping, he found her, huddled and barely conscious, in his sheepskin jacket. Barefoot.

He lifted her, heedless of the tears falling like crystalline drops across his cheeks. She whispered something—it sounded like his name—and burrowed closer.

By the time Flynn reached the cabin the last of the light was gone, faded to a velvety night. The storm was ebbing, snow fell gently now, while inside, the fire still crackled. He laid Constance on the couch in front of it and set about massaging her feet. He kept that up until she whimpered in protest and tried to pull away.

"Hold on, sweetheart," he said. "I've got to heat up some water. I'll be right back."

He needed to heat water to warm her feet slowly and steadily. But Constance had other ideas. She clung to him and reached a hand up unsteadily to touch his face.

"Oh, Flynn," she murmured brokenly, "I thought..."

"I know," he said, unable to hear her say what he knew was uppermost in her mind. It had been far too close a call, closer than he would ever want to experience again.

"Everything's all right now," he said. "I just have to..."

"No," she said, "don't go. I need you so much I—" She raised her head, azure eyes meeting his. ' love you, Flynn. I really do. It isn't just the fear anything like that. I realized out in the snow how much of what we think is important doesn't matter at all. Sheffield—"

Flynn covered her hands with his. "Damn it, I forgot all about him. Where is he? I—"

"Stop," she said. "Forget about him. He doesn't exist as far as we're concerned."

"He chased you out into that storm. If anything had happened to you, he would have been responsible."

She smiled gently, overwhelmed by what she saw in his gaze. "Nothing did, at least not if my feet are anything to go by. They're complaining with all they've got, so they must be all right."

He laughed despite himself. She loved him, she'd said so. And he loved her, God help him, because he'd never felt so vulnerable in his life. He'd better get used to it, though, because that wasn't going to change, not ever.

He had to call Morgenstern, warn him about Sheffield, there would be a million questions. But first—

"One thing, sweetheart," he said gently, "promise me you'll give up running around barefoot?"

"I promise!"

"Except in the summer, of course. You'll love it here then. We'll swim in that pool you found, lie around on the grass, maybe pick a few blackberries."

"Hmm, could we get back to the lying-around part again?"

"You like that idea?"

Her arms twined around his neck, drawing him to her. "Do we have to wait until summer?"

He frowned. "No, but we do have to take care of your feet first."

"That's what I always say, take care of your feet and your feet will take care of you."

"Idiot," he said fondly.

"Hmm, must be." Her eyelids were growing heavy despite a valiant effort to stay awake, if only to convince Flynn that there were better things to do than worry about her feet. After all, she could feel them again. What more did he want?

A great deal, as it turned out. First there was a long, warm bath, followed by a brisk toweling in what felt like a terry-cloth blanket, then a ride in his arms to the wide, welcoming bed.

The clouds were clearing. Moonlight shone silver on the snow. She watched as he stripped, dark and lean, and came to her. The bed sank under his weight. He was shaking with the force of his own desire and his relief in the aftermath of all that had happened. He dragged her into his arms and held her tightly, his head muffled against her shoulder.

She touched him then, gently and slowly. Beneath her hands and mouth, the fear fled. Only the passion and the love remained, surrounding and encompassing them both, taking them out of darkness into the light everlasting.

Epilogue

Ben Morgenstern's meeting with the mayor was short and to the point. "Elizabeth Sheffield is leaving town," the mayor announced. "She wants to put the whole unfortunate business of her son's death behind her."

"How come?" Ben asked. He was lighting one of the mayor's good cigars, the kind he kept in a humidor the size of a walk-in closet and handed out like gold.

"What do you mean, how come?" The mayor sighed with the forbearance required for holding any public office in New York and looked up at the ceiling.

"Lewis is old news. Rumor has it Charles isn't doing too well. Something about being found wandering along a highway in Connecticut in a snowstorm babbling about a guy wanting to hurt him. He had to be hospitalized in one of those country club places for rich weirdos. Seems like he's gonna be out of circulation for a while. A *long* while.''

Ben raised an eyebrow, the only acknowledgment he'd make that this wasn't exactly a surprise. He had talked with Flynn. "Oh, really? Gee, I wonder what could have happened to him."

The mayor removed his gaze from the ornately carved ceiling and leveled it at the district attorney. "You know damn well what. I had Corbett in here first thing this morning." He shook his head. "My God, what a mess. To think of those people with all their money and both of the sons screwed up like that."

He sounded genuinely disturbed, which was understandable since his own children were the pride of his life.

"Too bad only one of them's dead," he groused, reverting to his more businesslike self. "When I think of the contributions I took from them, if it ever comes out about Lewis and that girl years ago or Charles's own part in making him so twisted..." He shook his head, envisioning the shrieking tabloid headlines the citizens of his fair city would lap up like mother's milk.

"It won't come out," Ben assured him matter-of-factly. "Too many people in this town took too much money from the Sheffields and gave them too much clout to risk airing their dirty linen in public. No Mrs. Sheffield, no grand jury. No grand jury, no story. Everything nice and quiet."

"Which is exactly how I want it," the mayor said, "and how I assured Corbett it would be. You'll release a statement this morning saying that the matter is closed, official ruling of accidental death. In another day or two, some union will strike or a bridge will collapse or the banks will threaten to downgrade our bond rating. Something'll happen to give everybody something new to think about."

"It always does," Ben said agreeably.

The two men smiled at each other in perfect, if wary understanding.

"Wanna play a little handball?" the mayor asked.

"Sounds good," Ben replied.

They left the office together. "What's this I hear about Flynn getting married?" the mayor asked as they got into the elevator.

"I heard that, too," Ben said.

"I'll send him some cigars."

"His fiancée's a voter."

"Oh, yeah. Okay, something else, silver, crystal, like that. Where's she from, anyway?"

"Ohio," Ben replied.

"Ohio," the mayor repeated. "Where's that again?"

Ben gestured vaguely in the general direction of the Hudson River and the country beyond. "Out there, west. You know."

The mayor nodded and promptly forgot about it. "Crystal," he said, deciding. "A punch bowl, maybe for when they get together with their kids and grandkids, years from now." He smiled nostalgically. "Miriam and I, we got one of those when we got married. Couldn't see any use for it back then but believe me, it's had plenty."

"They'd like that," Ben said.

He was right, they did.

*   *   *   *   *

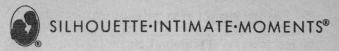

SILHOUETTE·INTIMATE·MOMENTS®

COMING
NEXT MONTH

#405   PROBABLE CAUSE—Marilyn Pappano

Strictly-by-the-book FBI agent Thad McNally had never gotten over his love for Lindsey Phillips. So when the case that had torn them apart was reopened, he didn't hesitate—he went to see her. But things got complicated when he realized that her life—as well as their love—was in danger.

#406   THE MAN NEXT DOOR—Alexandra Sellers

Hot on the trail of an international smuggling ring, police officer Sunny Delancey's low profile was nearly compromised when a mischievous cat got her entangled with the infamous Jock Prentiss. Yet being front-page news proved to be an advantage Sunny couldn't pass up, especially since being considered this hunk's latest lover was no hardship!

#407   TAKING SIDES—Lucy Hamilton

Determined to clear her father's reputation, faithful daughter Hope Carruthers confronted Sean Boudreaux, the only man who could set the record straight. Yet when searching for the truth demanded working closely with sexy Sean, Hope's heart discovered a different sort of truth altogether.

#408   ANGEL ON MY SHOULDER—Ann Williams

Cynical Will Alexander had no idea who the cupcake with the big blue eyes was—she claimed to be Cassandra, his guardian angel—but there was no way *anyone*, not even a woman as enticing as Cassandra, would stop him from getting revenge against his enemy. But he hadn't counted on Cassandra's heavenly means of persuasion....

AVAILABLE THIS MONTH:

#401   DESERT SHADOWS
Emilie Richards

#402   STEVIE'S CHASE
Justine Davis

#403   FORBIDDEN
Catherine Palmer

**#404   SIR FLYNN AND
LADY CONSTANCE**
Maura Seger

"INDULGE A LITTLE" SWEEPSTAKES

HERE'S HOW THE SWEEPSTAKES WORKS

NO PURCHASE NECESSARY

To enter each drawing, complete the appropriate Official Entry Form or a 3" by 5" index card by hand-printing your name, address and phone number and the trip destination that the entry is being submitted for (i.e., Walt Disney World Vacation Drawing, etc.) and mailing it to: Indulge '91 Subscribers-Only Sweepstakes, P.O. Box 1397, Buffalo, New York 14269-1397.

No responsibility is assumed for lost, late or misdirected mail. Entries must be sent separately with first class postage affixed, and be received by: 9/30/91 for the Walt Disney World Vacation Drawing, 10/31/91 for the Alaskan Cruise Drawing and 11/30/91 for the Hawaiian Vacation Drawing. Sweepstakes is open to residents of the U.S. and Canada, 21 years of age or older as of 11/7/91.

For complete rules, send a self-addressed, stamped (WA residents need not affix return postage) envelope to: Indulge '91 Subscribers-Only Sweepstakes Rules, P.O. Box 4005, Blair, NE 68009.

DIR-RL

"INDULGE A LITTLE" SWEEPSTAKES

HERE'S HOW THE SWEEPSTAKES WORKS

NO PURCHASE NECESSARY

To enter each drawing, complete the appropriate Official Entry Form or a 3" by 5" index card by hand-printing your name, address and phone number and the trip destination that the entry is being submitted for (i.e., Walt Disney World Vacation Drawing, etc.) and mailing it to: Indulge '91 Subscribers-Only Sweepstakes, P.O. Box 1397, Buffalo, New York 14269-1397.

No responsibility is assumed for lost, late or misdirected mail. Entries must be sent separately with first class postage affixed, and be received by: 9/30/91 for the Walt Disney World Vacation Drawing, 10/31/91 for the Alaskan Cruise Drawing and 11/30/91 for the Hawaiian Vacation Drawing. Sweepstakes is open to residents of the U.S. and Canada, 21 years of age or older as of 11/7/91.

For complete rules, send a self-addressed, stamped (WA residents need not affix return postage) envelope to: Indulge '91 Subscribers-Only Sweepstakes Rules, P.O. Box 4005, Blair, NE 68009.

© 1991 HARLEQUIN ENTERPRISES LTD. DIR-RL

INDULGE A LITTLE—WIN A LOT!

Summer of '91 Subscribers-Only Sweepstakes

OFFICIAL ENTRY FORM

This entry must be received by: Oct. 31, 1991
This month's winner will be notified by: Nov. 7, 1991
Trip must be taken between: May 27, 1992—Sept. 9, 1992
(depending on sailing schedule)

YES, I want to win the Alaska Cruise vacation for two. I understand the prize includes round-trip airfare, one-week cruise including private cabin, all meals and pocket money as revealed on the "wallet" scratch-off card.

Name _____

Address_____ Apt. _____

City _____

State/Prov. _____ Zip/Postal Code _____

Daytime phone number _____
(Area Code)

Return entries with invoice in envelope provided. Each book in this shipment has two entry coupons—and the more coupons you enter, the better your chances of winning!

© 1991 HARLEQUIN ENTERPRISES LTD.   2N-CPS

INDULGE A LITTLE—WIN A LOT!

Summer of '91 Subscribers-Only Sweepstakes

OFFICIAL ENTRY FORM

This entry must be received by: Oct. 31, 1991
This month's winner will be notified by: Nov. 7, 1991
Trip must be taken between: May 27, 1992—Sept. 9, 1992
(depending on sailing schedule)

YES, I want to win the Alaska Cruise vacation for two. I understand the prize includes round-trip airfare, one-week cruise including private cabin, all meals and pocket money as revealed on the "wallet" scratch-off card.

Name _____

Address_____ Apt. _____

City _____

State/Prov. _____ Zip/Postal Code _____

Daytime phone number _____
(Area Code)

Return entries with invoice in envelope provided. Each book in this shipment has two entry coupons—and the more coupons you enter, the better your chances of winning!

© 1991 HARLEQUIN ENTERPRISES LTD.   2N-CPS